The Short Stories Of William Makepeace Thackeray

The short story is often viewed as an inferior relation to the Novel. But it is an art in itself. To take a story and distil its essence into fewer pages while keeping character and plot rounded and driven is not an easy task. Many try and many fail.

In this series we look at short stories from many of our most accomplished writers. Miniature masterpieces with a lot to say. In this volume we examine some of the short stories of William Makepeace Thackeray.

The great author of Vanity Fair and The Luck Of Barry Lyndon was born in India in 1811. At age 5 his father died and his mother sent him back to England. His education was of the best but he himself seemed unable to apply his talents to a rigorous work ethic.

After a few years of marriage his wife began to suffer from depression and over the years became detached from reality. He himself suffered from ill health later in his life and the one pursuit that kept him moving forward was that of writing and in his life time he was placed second only to Dickens. High praise indeed.

In this volume we take some of his shorter works, they are perfect miniatures of the world as he saw it.

Many of these stories are also available as an audiobook from our sister company Word Of Mouth. Many samples are at our youtube channel http://www.youtube.com/user/PortablePoetry?feature=mhee The full volume can be purchased from iTunes, Amazon and other digital stores. They are read for you by Richard Mitchley & Ghizela Rowe

Index Of Titles
On Some Dinners At Paris
On Some Old Customs Of The Dinner Table
Mrs. Perkins's Ball
The Notch On The Ax

On Some Dinners At Paris

Some few words about dinners, my dear friend, I know your benevolent mind will expect. A man who comes to Paris without directing his mind to dinners, is like a fellow who travels to Athens without caring to inspect ruins, or an individual who goes to the Opera, and misses Jenny Lind's singing. No, I should be ungrateful to that appetite with which Nature has bountifully endowed me — to those recollections which render a consideration of the past so exquisite an enjoyment to me—were I to think of coming to Paris without enjoying a few quiet evenings at the Trois Fréres, alone, with a few dishes, a faithful waiter who knows me of old, and my own thoughts; undisturbed by conversation, or having to help the soup, or carve the turkey for the lady of the house; by the exertion of telling jokes for the entertainment of the company; by the ennui of a stupid neighbour at your side, to whom you are forced to impart them; by the disgust of hearing an opposition wag talk better than yourself, take the stories with which you have come primed and loaded out of your very mouth, and fire them off himself, or audaciously bring forward old Joe Millers, and get a laugh from all the company, when your own novelties and neatest impromptus and mots pass round the table utterly disregarded.

I rejoiced, Sir, in my mind, to think that I should be able to dine alone; without rivals to talk me out, hosts or ladies to coax and wheedle, or neighbours who, before my eyes (as they often have done), will take the best cutlet or favourite snipe out of the dish, as it is handed round, or to whom you have to give all the breast of the pheasant or capon, when you carve it.

All the way in the railroad, and through the tedious hours of night, I whiled away such time as I did not employ in sleeping, or in thinking about Miss Br-wn (who felt, I think, by the way, some little pang in parting with me, else why was she so silent all night, and why did she apply her pocket-handkerchief so constantly to her lovely amethyst eyes?)—all the way in the railroad, I say, when not occupied by other thoughts, I amused the tedium of the journey by inventing little bills of fare for one,—solitary Barmecide banquets,— which I enjoyed in spirit, and proposed to discuss bodily on my arrival in the Capital of the Kitchen.

"Monsieur will dine at the table d'hôte*?" the laquais de place said at the hotel, whilst I was arranging my elegant toilette before stepping forth to renew an acquaintance with our beloved old city. An expression of scornful incredulity shot across the fine features of the person addressed by the laquais de place. My fine fellow, thought I, do you think I am come to Paris in order to dine at a table d'hôte?—to meet twenty-four doubtful English and Americans at an ordinary?

"Lucullus dines with Lucullus to-day, Sir;" which, as the laquais de place did not understand, I added, "I never dine at table d'hôte, except at an extremity."

I had arranged in my mind a little quiet week of dinners. Twice or thrice, thinks I, I will dine at the Fréres, once at Véry's, once at the Café de Paris. If my old friend Voisin opposite the Assomption has some of the same sort of Bordeaux which we recollect in 1844, I will dine there at least twice. Philippe's, in the Rue Montorgueil, must be tried, which, they say, is as good as the Rocher de Cancale used to be in our time: and the seven days were chalked out already, and I saw there was nothing for it but to breakfast à la fourchette at some of the other places which I had in my mind, if I wished to revisit all my old haunts.

To a man living much in the world, or surrounded by his family, there is nothing so good as this solitude from time to time—there is nothing like communing with your own heart, and giving a calm and deliberate judgment upon the great question—the truly vital question, I may say—before you. What is the use of having your children, who live on roast mutton in the nursery, and think treacle-pudding the summit of cookery, to sit down and take the best three-fourths of a perdreau truffé with you? What is the use of helping your wife, who doesn't know the difference between sherry and madeira, to a glass of priceless Romanée or sweetly odoriferous Château Lafitte of '42? Poor dear soul! she would be as happy with a slice of the children's joint, and a cup of tea in the evening. She takes them when you are away. To give fine wine to that dear creature is like giving pearls to—to animals who don't know their value.

What I like, is to sit at a restaurant alone, after having taken a glass of absinthe in water, about half-an-hour previous, to muse well over the carte, and pick out some little dinner for myself; to converse with the sommelier confidentially about the wine—a pint of Champagne, say, and a bottle of Bordeaux, or a bottle of Burgundy, not more, for your private drinking. He goes out to satisfy your wishes, and returns with the favourite flask in a cradle, very likely. Whilst he is gone, comes old Antoine—who is charmed to see Monsieur de retour; and vows that you rajeunissez tous les ans—with a plate of oysters—dear little juicy green oysters in their upper shells, swimming in their sweet native brine—not like your great white flaccid natives in England, that look as if they had been fed on pork: and ah! how kindly and pretty that attention is of the two little plates of radishes and butter, which they bring you in, and with which you can dally between the arrival of the various dishes of your dinner; they are like the delicate symphonies which are played at the theatre between the acts of a charming comedy. A little bread-and-butter, a little radish,—you crunch and relish; a little radish, a little piece of bread and-butter—you relish and crunch—when lo! up goes the curtain, and Antoine comes in with the entrée or the roast.

I pictured all this in my mind and went out. I will not tell any of my friends that I am here, thought I. Sir, in five minutes, and before I had crossed the Place Vendôme, I had met five old acquaintances and friends, and in an hour afterwards the arrival of your humble servant was known to all our old set.

My first visit was for Tom Dash, with whom I had business. That friend.of my youth received me with the utmost cordiality: and our business transacted and our acquaintances talked over (four of them I had seen, so that it was absolutely necessary I should call on them and on the rest), it was agreed that I should go forth and pay visits, and that on my return Tom and I should dine somewhere together. I called upon Brown, upon Jones, upon Smith, upon Robinson, upon our old Paris set, in a word, and in due time returned to Tom Dash.

"Where are we to dine, Tom ?" says I. "What is the crack restaurant now? I am entirely in your hands; and let us be off early and go to the play afterwards."

"Oh, hang restaurants," says Tom—"I'm tired of 'em; we are sick of them here. Thompson came in just after you were gone, and I told him you were coming, and he will be here directly to have a chop with me."

There was nothing for it. I had to sit down and dine with Thompson and Tom Dash, at the latter's charges—and am bound to say that the dinner was not a bad one. As I have said somewhere before, and am proud of being able to say, I scarcely recollect ever to have had a bad dinner.

But of what do you think the present repast was composed? Sir, I give you my honour, we had a slice of salmon and a leg of mutton, and boiled potatoes, just as they do in my favourite Baker Street.

"Dev'lish good dinner," says Thompson, covering the salmon with lots of Harvey sauce — and cayenne pepper, from Fortnum and Mason's.

"Donnez du sherry à Monsieur Canterbury," says Tom Dash to Francois his man. "There's porter or pale ale if any man likes it."

They poured me out sherry; I might have had porter or pale ale if I liked: I had leg of mutton and potatoes, and finished dinner with Stilton cheese: and it was for this that I have revisited my dear Paris.

"Thank you," says I to Dash, cutting into the mutton with the most bitter irony.

"This is a dish that I don't remember ever having seen in England; but I tasted pale ale there, and won't take any this evening, thank you. Are we going to have port wine after dinner? or could you oblige me with a little London gin-and-water?"

Tom Dash laughed his mighty laugh; and I will say we had not port wine, but claret, fit for the repast of a pontiff, after dinner, and sat over it so late that the theatre was impossible, and the first day was gone, and might as well have been passed in Pump Court or Pall Mall, for all the good I had out of it.

But, Sir, do you know what had happened in the morning of that day during which I was paying the visits before mentioned?

Robinson, my very old friend, pressed me so to come and dine with him, and fix my day, that I could not refuse, and fixed Friday.

Brown, who is very rich, and with whom I had had a difference, insisted so upon our meeting as in old times, that I could not refuse; and so being called on to appoint my own day—I selected Sunday.

Smith is miserably poor, and it would offend him and Mrs. Smith mortally that I should dine with a rich man, and turn up my nose at his kind and humble table. I was free to name any day I liked, and so I chose Monday.

Meanwhile, our old friend Jones had heard that I had agreed to dine with Brown, with whom he, too, was at variance, and he offered downright to quarrel with me unless I gave him a day: so I fixed Thursday.

"I have but Saturday," says I, with almost tears in my eyes.

"Oh, I have asked a party of the old fellows to meet you," cries out Tom Dash; "and made a dinner expressly for the occasion."

And this, Sir, was the fact. This was the way, Sir, that I got my dinners at Paris. Sir, at one house I had boiled leg of mutton and turnips, at another beefsteak; and I give you my word of honour, at two I had mock-turtle soup! In this manner I saw Paris. This was what my friends called welcoming me — we drank sherry; we talked about Mr. Cobden and the new financial reform; I was not allowed to see a single Frenchman, save one, a huge athletic monster, whom I saw at a club in London, last year, who speaks English as well as you, and who drank two bottles of port wine on that very night for his own share. I offended mortally several old friends with whom I didn't dine, and I might as well have been sitting under your mahogany tree in Fleet Street, for all of Paris that I saw.

I have the honour to report my return to this country, and to my lodgings in Piccadilly, and to remain

> Your very obedient servant and
> contributor,
> Folkstone Canterbury.

P.S. — I stop the post to give the following notice from the Constitutionnel: — "Lady Jane Grey (femme du Chancelier de l'Echiquier) vient de donner le jour à deux jumeaux. Sa santé est aussi satisfaisante que possible."

*table d'hôte: a restaurant meal offered at a fixed price and with few if any choices.
ORIGIN early 17th cent.: French, literally 'host's table.' The term originally denoted a table in a hotel or restaurant where all guests ate together, hence a meal served there at a stated time and for a fixed price.

On Some Old Customs Of The Dinner Table

Of all the sciences which have made a progress in late years, I think, dear Bob (to return to the subject from which I parted with so much pleasure last week), that the art of dinner-giving has made the most delightful and rapid advances. Sir, I maintain, even now with a matured age and appetite, that the dinners of this present day are better than those we had in our youth, and I can't but be thankful at least once in every day for this decided improvement in our civilization. Those who remember the usages of five-and-twenty years back will be ready, I am sure, to acknowledge this progress. I was turning over at the club yesterday a queer little book written at that period, which, I believe, had some authority at the time, and which records some of those customs which obtained, if not in good London society, at least in some companies, and parts of our islands. Sir, many of these practices seem as antiquated now as the usages described in the accounts of Homeric feasts, or Queen Elizabeth's banquets and breakfasts. Let us be happy to think they are gone.

The book in question is called 'The Maxims of Sir Morgan O'Doherty,' a queer baronet, who appears to have lived in the first quarter of the century, and whose opinions the antiquarian may examine, not without profit—a strange barbarian indeed it is, and one wonders that such customs should ever have been prevalent in our country.

Fancy such opinions as these having ever been holden by any set of men among us: Maxim 2.—'It is laid down in fashionable life that yon must drink champagne after white cheeses, water after red. . . Ale is to be avoided in case a wet night is to be expected, as should cheese also. 'Maxim 4. —'A fine singer, after dinner, is to be avoided, for he is a great bore, and stops the wine… One of the best rules (to put him down) is to applaud him most vociferously as soon as he has sung the first verse, as if all was over, and say to the gentleman farthest from you at table that you admire the conclusion of this song very much. 'Maxim 25.—'You meet people occasionally who tell you it is bad taste to give champagne at dinner—port and teneriffe being such superior drinkmg,' etc., etc.

I am copying out of a book printed three months since, describing ways prevalent when you were born. Can it be possible, I say, that England was ever in such a state?

Was it ever a maxim in 'fashionable life' that you were to drink champagne after white cheeses? What was that maxim in fashionable life about drinking and about cheese? The maxim in fashionable life is to drink what you will. It is too simple now to trouble itself about wine or about cheese. Ale, again, is to be avoided, this strange Doherty says, if you expect a wet night—and in another place he says 'the English drink a pint of porter at a draught. 'What English? gracious powers! Are we a nation of coal heavers? Do we ever have a wet night? Do we ever meet people occasionally who say that to give champagne at dinner is bad taste, and that port and teneriffe are such superior drinking? Fancy teneriffe, my dear boy—I say fancy a man asking you to drink teneriffe at dinner; the mind shudders at it—he might as well invite you to swallow the Peak.

And then consider the maxim about the fine singer who is to be avoided. What! was there a time in most people's memory when folks at dessert began to sing? I have heard such a thing at a tenants' dinner in the country; but the idea of a fellow beginning to perform a song at a dinner party in London fills my mind with terror and amazement; and I picture to myself any table which I frequent, in May Fair, in Bloomsbury, in Belgravia, or where you will, and the pain which would seize upon the host and the company if some wretch were to commence a song.

We have passed that savage period of life. We do not want to hear songs from guests—we have the songs done for us—as we don't want our ladies to go down into the kitchen and cook the dinner any more. The cook can do it better and cheaper. We do not desire feats of musical or culinary skill— but simple, quiet, easy, unpretending conversation.

In like manner, there was a practice once usual, and which still lingers here and there, of making complimentary speeches after diuner; that custom is happily almost entirely discontinued. Gentlemen do not meet to compliment each other profusely, or to make fine phrases. Simplicity gains upon us daily. Let us be thankful that the florid style is disappearing.

I once shared a bottle of sherry with a commercial traveler at Margate who gave a toast or a sentiment as he filled every glass. He would not take his wine without this queer ceremony before it. I recollect one of his sentiments, which was as follows: 'Year is to 'er that doubles our joys, and divides our sorrows—I give woman, sir'—and we both emptied our glasses. These lumbering ceremonials are passing out of our manners, and were found only to obstruct our free intercourse. People can like each other just as much without orations, and be just as merry without being forced to drink against their will.

And yet there are certain customs to which one clings still; for instance, the practice of drinking wine with your neighbor, though wisely not so frequently indulged in as of old, yet still obtains, and I trust will never be abolished. For though, in the old time, when Mr. and Mrs. Fogy had sixteen friends to dinner, it became an unsupportable corvée for Mr. F. to ask sixteen persons to drink wine, and a painful task for Mrs. Fogy to be called upon to bow to ten gentlemen, who desired to have the honor to drink her health, yet, employed in moderation, that ancient custom of challenging your friends to drink is a kindly and hearty old usage, and productive of many most beneficial results.

I have known a man of a modest and reserved turn (just like your old uncle, dear Bob, as no doubt you were going to remark), when asked to drink by the host, suddenly lighten up, toss off his glass, get confidence, and begin to talk right and left. He wanted but the spur to set him going. It is supplied by the butler at the back of his chair.

It sometimes happens, again, that a host's conversational powers are not brilliant. I own that I could point out a few such whom I have the honor to name among my friends— gentlemen, in fact, who wisely hold their tongues because they have nothing to say which is worth the hearing or the telling, and properly confine themselves to the carving of the mutton and the ordering of the wines. Such men, manifestly, should always be allowed, nay, encouraged, to ask their guests to take wine. In putting that question, they show their good will, and cannot possibly betray their mental deficiency. For example, let us suppose Jones, who has been perfectly silent all dinner time, oppressed, doubtless, by that awful Lady Tiara, who sits swelling on his right hand, suddenly rallies, singles me out, and with a loud cheering voice cries, 'Brown, my boy, a glass of wine.' I reply, 'With pleasure, my dear Jones.' He responds as quick as thought, 'Shall it be hock or champagne, Brown?' I mention the wine which I prefer. He calls to the butler, and says, 'Some champagne or hock' (as the case may be, for I don't choose to commit myself)— 'some champagne or hock to Mr. Brown'; and finally he says, 'Good health!' in a pleasant tone. Thus you see, Jones, though not a conversationalist, has had the opportunity of making no less than four observations, which, if not brilliant or witty, are yet manly, sensible, and agreeable. And I defy any man in the metropolis, be he the most accomplished, the most learned, the wisest, or the most eloquent, to say more than Jones upon a similar occasion.

If you have had a difference with a man, and are desirous to make it up, how pleasant it is to take wine with him. Nothing is said but that simple phrase which has just been uttered by my friend Jones; and yet it means a great deal. The cup is a symbol of reconciliation. The other party drinks up your good will as you accept his token of returning friendship—and thus the liquor is hallowed which Jones has paid for; and I like to think that the grape which grew by Rhine or Rhone was born and ripened under the sun there, so as to be the means of bringing two good fellows together. I once heard the head physician of a hydropathic establishment on the sunny banks of the first-named river, give the health of his Majesty the King of Prussia, and calling upon the company to receive that august toast with a 'donnerndes Lebehoch,' toss off a bumper of sparkling water. It did not seem to me a genuine enthusiasm. No, no; let us have toast and wine, not toast and water. It was not in vain that grapes grew on the hills of Father Rhine.

One seldom asks ladies now to take wine—except when, in a confidential whisper to the charming creature whom you have brought down to dinner, you humbly ask permission to pledge her, and she delicately touches her glass with a fascinating smile, in reply to your glance—a smile, you rogue, which goes to your heart. I say, one does not ask ladies anymore to take wine; and I think, this custom being abolished, the contrary practice should be introduced, and that the ladies should ask the gentlemen. I know one who did, une grande dame de par le monde, as honest Brantome phrases it, and from whom I deserved no such kindness; but, sir, the effect of that graceful act of hospitality was such that she made a grateful slave forever of one who was an admiring rebel previously, who would do anything to show his gratitude, and who now knows no greater delight than when he receives a card which bears her respected name.

A dinner of men is well now and again, but few well-regulated minds relish a dinner without women. There are some wretches who, I believe, still meet together for the sake of what is called 'the spread,' who dine each other round and round, and have horrid delights in turtle, early pease, and other culinary luxuries—but I pity the condition as I avoid the banquets of those men. The only substitute for ladies at dinners, or consolation for want of them, is—smoking. Cigars, introduced with the coffee, do, if anything can, make us forget the absence of the other sex. But what a substitute is that for her who doubles our joys, and divides our griefs! for woman! as my friend the traveler said.

A Little Dinner At Timmin's

1

Mr. and Mrs. Fitzroy Timmins live in Lilliput Street, that neat little street which runs at right angles with the Park and Brobdingnag Gardens. It is a very genteel neighborhood, and I need not say they are of a good family.

Especially Mrs. Timmins, as her mamma is always telling Mr. T. They are Suffolk people, and distantly related to the Right honorable the Earl of Bungay.

Besides his house in Lilliput Street, Mr. Timmins has chambers in Fig-tree Court, Temple, and goes the Northern Circuit.

The other day, when there was a slight difference about the payment of fees between the great Parliamentary Counsel and the Solicitors, Stoke and Pogers, of Great George Street, sent the papers of the Lough Foyle and Lough Corrib Junction Railway to Mr. Fitzroy Timmins, who was so elated that he instantly purchased a couple of looking-glasses for his drawing-rooms (the front room is 16 by 12, and the back, a tight but elegant apartment, 10 ft. 6 by 8 ft. 4), a coral for the baby, two new dresses for Mrs. Timmins, and a little rosewood desk, at the Pantechnicon, for which Rosa had long been sighing, with crumpled legs, emerald-green and gold morocco top, and drawers all over.

Mrs. Timmins is a very pretty poetess (her "Lines to a Faded Tulip" and her "Plaint of Plinlimmon" appeared in one of last year's Keepsakes); and Fitzroy, as he impressed a kiss on the snowy forehead of his bride, pointed out to her, in one of the innumerable pockets of the desk, an elegant ruby-tipped pen, and six charming little gilt blank books, marked "My Books," which Mrs. Fitzroy might fill, he said, (he is an Oxford man, and very polite,) "with the delightful productions of her Muse." Besides these books, there was pink paper, paper with crimson edges, lace paper, all stamped with R. F. T. (Rosa Fitzroy Timmins) and the hand and battle-axe, the crest of the Timminses (and borne at Ascalon by Roaldus de Timmins, a crusader, who is now buried in the Temple Church, next to Serjeant Snooks), and yellow, pink, light-blue and other scented sealing waxes, at the service of Rosa when she chose to correspond with her friends.

Rosa, you may be sure, jumped with joy at the sight of this sweet present; called her Charles (his first name is Samuel, but they have sunk that) the best of men; embraced him a great number of times, to the edification of her buttony little page, who stood at the landing; and as soon as he was gone to chambers, took the new pen and a sweet sheet of paper, and began to compose a poem.

"What shall it be about?" was naturally her first thought. "What should be a young mother's first inspiration?" Her child lay on the sofa asleep before her; and she began in her neatest hand-
"LINES

"ON MY SON BUNGAY DE BRACY GASHLEIGH TYMMYNS, AGED TEN MONTHS.
"Tuesday.
"How beautiful! how beautiful thou seemest,
My boy, my precious one, my rosy babe!
Kind angels hover round thee, as thou dreamest,
Soft lashes hide thy beauteous azure eye which gleamest."

"Gleamest? thine eye which gleamest? Is that grammar?" thought Rosa, who had puzzled her little brains for some time with this absurd question, when the baby woke. Then the cook came up to ask about dinner; then Mrs. Fundy slipped over from No. 27 (they are opposite neighbors, and made an acquaintance through Mrs. Fundy's macaw); and a thousand things happened. Finally, there was no rhyme to babe except Tippoo Saib (against whom Major Gashleigh, Rosa's grandfather, had distinguished himself), and so she gave up the little poem about her De Bracy.

Nevertheless, when Fitzroy returned from chambers to take a walk with his wife in the Park, as he peeped through the rich tapestry hanging which divided the two drawing-rooms, he found his dear girl still seated at the desk, and writing, writing away with her ruby pen as fast as it could scribble.

"What a genius that child has!" he said; "why, she is a second Mrs. Norton!" and advanced smiling to peep over her shoulder and see what pretty thing Rosa was composing.

It was not poetry, though, that she was writing, and Fitz read as follows:-
"LILLIPUT STREET, Tuesday, 22nd May.

"Mr. and Mr. Fitzroy Tymmyns request the pleasure of Sir Thomas and Lady Kicklebury's company at dinner on Wednesday, at 7 1/2 o'clock."

"My dear!" exclaimed the barrister, pulling a long face.

"Law, Fitzroy!" cried the beloved of his bosom, "how you do startle one!"

"Give a dinner-party with our means!" said he.

"Ain't you making a fortune, you miser?" Rosa said. "Fifteen guineas a day is four thousand five hundred a year; I've calculated it." And, so saying, she rose and taking hold of his whiskers (which are as fine as those of any man of his circuit,) she put her mouth close up against his and did something to his long face, which quite changed the expression of it; and which the little page heard outside the door.

"Our dining-room won't hold ten," he said.

"We'll only ask twenty, my love. Ten are sure to refuse in this season, when everybody is giving parties. Look, here is the list."

"Earl and Countess of Bungay, and Lady Barbara Saint Mary's."

"You are dying to get a lord into the house," Timmins said (HE had not altered his name in Fig-tree Court yet, and therefore I am not so affected as to call him TYMMYNS).

"Law, my dear, they are our cousins, and must be asked," Rosa said.

"Let us put down my sister and Tom Crowder, then."

"Blanche Crowder is really so VERY fat, Fitzroy," his wife said, "and our rooms are so VERY small."

Fitz laughed. "You little rogue," he said, "Lady Bungay weighs two of Blanche, even when she's not in the f-"

"Fiddlesticks!" Rose cried out. "Doctor Crowder really cannot be admitted: he makes such a noise eating his soup, that it is really quite disagreeable." And she imitated the gurgling noise performed by the Doctor while inhausting his soup, in such a funny way that Fitz saw inviting him was out of the question.

"Besides, we mustn't have too many relations," Rosa went on. "Mamma, of course, is coming. She doesn't like to be asked in the evening; and she'll bring her silver bread-basket and her candlesticks, which are very rich and handsome."

"And you complain of Blanche for being too stout!" groaned out Timmins.

"Well, well, don't be in a pet," said little Rosa. "The girls won't come to dinner; but will bring their music afterwards." And she went on with the list.

"Sir Thomas and Lady Kicklebury, 2. No saying no: we MUST ask them, Charles. They are rich people, and any room in their house in Brobdingnag Gardens would swallow up OUR humble cot. But to people in OUR position in SOCIETY they will be glad enough to come. The city people are glad to mix with the old families."

"Very good," says Fitz, with a sad face of assent and Mrs. Timmins went on reading her list.

"Mr. and Mrs. Topham Sawyer, Belgravine Place."

"Mrs. Sawyer hasn't asked you all the season. She gives herself the airs of an empress; and when-"

"One's Member, you know, my dear, one must have," Rosa replied, with much dignity as if the presence of the representative of her native place would be a protection to her dinner. And a note was written and transported by the page early next morning to the mansion of the Sawyers, in Belgravine Place.

The Topham Sawyers had just come down to breakfast; Mrs. T. in her large dust-colored morning-dress and Madonna front (she looks rather scraggy of a morning, but I promise you her ringlets and figure will stun you of an evening); and having read the note, the following dialogue passed:--

Mrs. Topham Sawyer.--"Well, upon my word, I don't know where things will end. Mr. Sawyer, the Timminses have asked us to dinner."

Mr. Topham Sawyer. "Ask us to dinner! What damn impudence!"

Mrs. Topham Sawyer.--"The most dangerous and insolent revolutionary principles are abroad, Mr. Sawyer; and I shall write and hint as much to these persons."

Mr. Topham Sawyer. "No, damn it, Joanna: they are my constituents and we must go. Write a civil note, and say we will come to their party." (He resumes the perusal of 'The times,' and Mrs. Topham Sawyer writes)

"MY DEAR ROSA,
We shall have GREAT PLEASURE in joining your little party. I do not reply in the third person, as WE ARE OLD FRIENDS, you know, and COUNTRY NEIGHBORS. I hope your mamma is well: present my KINDEST REMEMBRANCES to her, and I hope we shall see much MORE of each other in the summer, when we go down to the Sawpits (for going abroad is out of the question in these DREADFUL TIMES). With a hundred kisses to your dear little PET,

"Believe me your attached
"J. T. S."

She said Pet, because she did not know whether Rosa's child was a girl or boy: and Mrs. Timmins was very much pleased with the kind and gracious nature of the reply to her invitation.

II.

The next persons whom little Mrs. Timmins was bent upon asking, were Mr. and Mrs. John Rowdy, of the firm of Stumpy, Rowdy and Co., of Brobdingnag Gardens, of the Prairie, Putney, and of Lombard Street, City.

Mrs. Timinins and Mrs. Rowdy had been brought up at the same school together, and there was always a little rivalry between them, from the day when they contended for the French prize at school to last week, when each had a stall at the Fancy Fair for the benefit of the Daughters of Decayed Muffin-men; and when Mrs. Timmins danced against Mrs. Rowdy in the Scythe Mazurka at the Polish Ball, headed by Mrs. Hugh Slasher. Rowdy took twenty-three pounds more than Timmins in the Muffin transaction (for she had possession of a kettle-holder worked by the hands of Royalty, which brought crowds to her stall); but in the Mazurka Rosa conquered: she has the prettiest little foot possible (which in a red boot and silver heel looked so lovely that even the Chinese ambassador remarked it), whereas Mrs. Rowdy's foot is no trifle, as Lord Cornbury acknowledged when it came down on his lordship's boot-tip as they danced together amongst the Scythes.

"These people are ruining themselves," said Mrs. John Rowdy to her husband, on receiving the pink note. It was carried round by that rogue of a buttony page in the evening; and he walked to Brobdingnag Gardens, and in the Park afterwards, with a young lady who is kitchen-maid at 27, and who is not more than fourteen years older than little Buttons.

"These people are ruining themselves," said Mrs. John to her husband. "Rosa says she has asked the Bungays."

"Bungays indeed! Timmins was always a tuft-hunter," said Rowdy, who had been at college with the barrister, and who, for his own part, has no more objection to a lord than you or I have; and adding,

"Hang him, what business has HE to be giving parties?" allowed Mrs. Rowdy, nevertheless, to accept Rosa's invitation.

"When I go to business to-morrow, I will just have a look at Mr. Fitz's account," Mr. Rowdy thought; "and if it is overdrawn, as it usually is, why . . ." The announcement of Mrs. Rowdy's brougham here put an end to this agreeable train of thought; and the banker and his lady stepped into it to join a snug little family-party of two-and-twenty, given by Mr. and Mrs. Secondchop at their great house on the other side of the Park.

"Rowdys 2, Bungays 3, ourselves and mamma 3, 2 Sawyers," calculated little Rosa.

"General Gulpin," Rosa continued, "eats a great deal, and is very stupid, but he looks well at table with his star and ribbon. Let us put HIM down!" and she noted down "Sir Thomas and Lady Gulpin, 2. Lord Castlemouldy, 1."

"You will make your party abominably genteel and stupid," groaned Timmins. "Why don't you ask some of our old friends? Old Mrs. Portman has asked us twenty times, I am sure, within the last two years."

"And the last time we went there, there was pea-soup for dinner!" Mrs. Timmins said, with a look of ineffable scorn.

"Nobody can have been kinder than the Hodges have always been to us; and some sort of return we might make, I think."

"Return, indeed! A pretty sound it is on the staircase to hear 'Mr. and Mrs. 'Odge and Miss 'Odges' pronounced by Billiter, who always leaves his h's out. No, no: see attorneys at your chambers, my dear--but what could the poor creatures do in OUR society?" And so, one by one, Timmins's old friends were tried and eliminated by Mrs. Timmins, just as if she had been an Irish Attorney-General, and they so many Catholics on Mr. Mitchel's jury.

Mrs. Fitzroy insisted that the party should be of her very best company. Funnyman, the great wit, was asked, because of his jokes; and Mrs. Butt, on whom he practises; and Potter, who is asked because everybody else asks him; and Mr. Ranville Ranville of the Foreign Office, who might give some news of the Spanish squabble; and Botherby, who has suddenly sprung up into note because he is intimate with the French Revolution, and visits Ledru-Rollin and Lamartine. And these, with a couple more who are amis de la maison, made up the twenty, whom Mrs. Timmins thought she might safely invite to her little dinner.

But the deuce of it was, that when the answers to the invitations came back, everybody accepted! Here was a pretty quandary. How they were to get twenty into their dining-room was a calculation which poor Timmins could not solve at all; and he paced up and down the little room in dismay.

"Pooh!" said Rosa with a laugh. "Your sister Blanche looked very well in one of my dresses last year; and you know how stout she is. We will find some means to accommodate them all, depend upon it."

Mrs. John Rowdy's note to dear Rosa, accepting the latter's invitation, was a very gracious and kind one; and Mrs. Fitz showed it to her husband when he came back from chambers. But there was another note which had arrived for him by this time from Mr. Rowdy--or rather from the firm; and to the effect that Mr. F. Timmins had overdrawn his account 28L. 18s. 6d., and was requested to pay that sum to his obedient servants, Stumpy, Rowdy and Co.

And Timmins did not like to tell his wife that the contending parties in the Lough Foyle and Lough Corrib Railroad had come to a settlement, and that the fifteen guineas a day had consequently determined. "I have had seven days of it, though," he thought; "and that will be enough to pay for the desk, the dinner, and the glasses, and make all right with Stumpy and Rowdy."

III.

The cards for dinner having been issued, it became the duty of Mrs. Timmins to make further arrangements respecting the invitations to the tea-party which was to follow the more substantial meal.

These arrangements are difficult, as any lady knows who is in the habit of entertaining her friends. There are People who are offended if you ask them to tea whilst others have been asked to dinner;

People who are offended if you ask them to tea at all; and cry out furiously, "Good heavens! Jane my love, why do these Timminses suppose that I am to leave my dinner-table to attend their ----- soiree?" (the dear reader may fill up the ----- to any strength, according to his liking) or, "Upon my word, William my dear, it is too much to ask us to pay twelve shillings for a brougham, and to spend I don't know how much in gloves, just to make our curtsies in Mrs. Timmins's little drawing-room." Mrs. Moser made the latter remark about the Timmins affair, while the former was uttered by Mr. Grumpley, barrister-at-law, to his lady, in Gloucester Place.

That there are people who are offended if you don't ask them at all, is a point which I suppose nobody will question. Timmins's earliest friend in life was Simmins, whose wife and family have taken a cottage at Mortlake for the season.

"We can't ask them to come out of the country," Rosa said to her Fitzroy (between ourselves, she was delighted that Mrs. Simmins was out of the way, and was as jealous of her as every well-regulated woman should be of her husband's female friends) "we can't ask them to come so far for the evening."

"Why, no, certainly." said Fitzroy, who has himself no very great opinion of a tea-party; and so the Simminses were cut out of the list.

And what was the consequence? The consequence was, that Simmins and Timmins cut when they met at Westminster; that Mrs. Simmins sent back all the books which she had borrowed from Rosa, with a withering note of thanks; that Rosa goes about saying that Mrs. Simmins squints; that Mrs. S., on her side, declares that Rosa is crooked, and behaved shamefully to Captain Hicks in marrying Fitzroy over him, though she was forced to do it by her mother, and prefers the Captain to her husband to this day. If, in a word, these two men could be made to fight, I believe their wives would not be displeased; and the reason of all this misery, rage, and dissension, lies in a poor little twopenny dinner-party in Lilliput Street.

Well, the guests, both for before and after meat, having been asked, old Mrs. Gashleigh, Rosa's mother (and, by consequence, Fitzroy's DEAR mother-in-law, though I promise you that "dear" is particularly sarcastic) Mrs. Gashleigh of course was sent for, and came with Miss Eliza Gashleigh, who plays on the guitar, and Emily, who limps a little, but plays sweetly on the concertina. They live close by--trust them for that. Your mother-in-law is always within hearing, thank our stars for the attention of the dear women. The Gashleighs, I say, live close by, and came early on the morning after Rosa's notes had been issued for the dinner.

When Fitzroy, who was in his little study, which opens into his little dining-room--one of those absurd little rooms which ought to be called a gentleman's pantry, and is scarcely bigger than a shower-bath, or a state cabin in a ship, when Fitzroy heard his mother-in-law's knock, and her well-known scuffling and chattering in the passage--in which she squeezed up young Buttons, the page, while she put questions to him regarding baby, and the cook's health, and whether she had taken what Mrs. Gashleigh had sent overnight, and the housemaid's health, and whether Mr. Timmins had gone to chambers or not and when, after this preliminary chatter, Buttons flung open the door, announcing "Mrs. Gashleigh and the young ladies," Fitzroy laid down his Times newspaper with an expression that had best not be printed here, and took his hat and walked away.

Mrs. Gashleigh has never liked him since he left off calling her mamma, and kissing her. But he said he could not stand it any longer he was hanged if he would. So he went away to chambers, leaving the field clear to Rosa, mamma, and the two dear girls.

Or to one of them, rather: for before leaving the house, he thought he would have a look at little Fitzroy up stairs in the nursery, and he found the child in the hands of his maternal aunt Eliza, who was holding him and pinching him as if he had been her guitar, I suppose; so that the little fellow bawled pitifully and his father finally quitted the premises.

No sooner was he gone, although the party was still a fortnight off, than the women pounced upon his little study, and began to put it in order. Some of his papers they pushed up over the bookcase, some they put behind the Encyclopaedia. Some they crammed into the drawers where Mrs. Gashleigh found three cigars, which she pocketed, and some letters, over which she cast her eye; and by Fitz's return they had the room as neat as possible, and the best glass and dessert-service mustered on the study table.

It was a very neat and handsome service, as you may be sure Mrs. Gashleigh thought, whose rich uncle had purchased it for the young couple, at Spode and Copeland's; but it was only for twelve persons.

It was agreed that it would be, in all respects, cheaper and better to purchase a dozen more dessert-plates; and with "my silver basket in the centre," Mrs. G. said (she is always bragging about that confounded bread-basket), "we need not have any extra china dishes, and the table will look very pretty."

On making a roll-call of the glass, it was calculated that at least a dozen or so tumblers, four or five dozen wines, eight water-bottles, and a proper quantity of ice-plates, were requisite; and that, as they would always be useful, it would be best to purchase the articles immediately. Fitz tumbled over the basket containing them, which stood in the hall as he came in from chambers, and over the boy who had brought them and the little bill.

The women had had a long debate, and something like a quarrel, it must be owned, over the bill of fare. Mrs. Gashleigh, who had lived a great part of her life in Devonshire, and kept house in great state there, was famous for making some dishes, without which, she thought, no dinner could be perfect. When she proposed her mock-turtle, and stewed pigeons, and gooseberry-cream, Rosa turned up her nose a pretty little nose it was, by the way, and with a natural turn in that direction.

"Mock-turtle in June, mamma!" said she.

"It was good enough for your grandfather, Rosa," the mamma replied: "it was good enough for the Lord High Admiral, when he was at Plymouth; it was good enough for the first men in the county, and relished by Lord Fortyskewer and Lord Rolls; Sir Lawrence Porker ate twice of it after Exeter races; and I think it might be good enough for-"

"I will NOT have it, mamma!" said Rosa, with a stamp of her foot; and Mrs. Gashleigh knew what resolution there was in that. Once, when she had tried to physic the baby, there had been a similar fight between them.

So Mrs. Gashleigh made out a carte, in which the soup was left with a dash, a melancholy vacuum; and in which the pigeons were certainly thrust in among the entrees; but Rosa determined they never should make an entree at all into HER dinner-party, but that she would have the dinner her own way.

When Fitz returned, then, and after he had paid the little bill of 6L. 14s. 6d. for the glass, Rosa flew to him with her sweetest smiles, and the baby in her arms. And after she had made him remark how the child grew every day more and more like him, and after she had treated him to a number of compliments and caresses, which it were positively fulsome to exhibit in public, and after she had soothed him into good humor by her artless tenderness, she began to speak to him about some little points which she had at heart.

She pointed out with a sigh how shabby the old curtains looked since the dear new glasses which her darling Fitz had given her had been put up in the drawing-room. Muslin curtains cost nothing, and she must and would have them.

The muslin curtains were accorded. She and Fitz went and bought them at Shoolbred's, when you may be sure she treated herself likewise to a neat, sweet pretty half-mourning (for the Court, you know, is in mourning) a neat sweet barege, or calimanco, or bombazine, or tiffany, or some such thing; but Madame Camille, of Regent Street, made it up, and Rosa looked like an angel in it on the night of her little dinner.

"And, my sweet," she continued, after the curtains had been accorded, "mamma and I have been talking about the dinner. She wants to make it very expensive, which I cannot allow. I have been thinking of a delightful and economical plan, and you, my sweetest Fitz, must put it into execution."

"I have cooked a mutton-chop when I was in chambers," Fitz said with a laugh. "Am I to put on a cap and an apron?"

"No: but you are to go to the 'Megatherium Club' (where, you wretch, you are always going without my leave), and you are to beg Monsieur Mirobolant, your famous cook, to send you one of his best aides-de-camp, as I know he will, and with his aid we can dress the dinner and the confectionery at home for ALMOST NOTHING, and we can show those purse-proud Topham Sawyers and Rowdys that the HUMBLE COTTAGE can furnish forth an elegant entertainment as well as the gilded halls of wealth."

Fitz agreed to speak to Monsieur Mirobolant. If Rosa had had a fancy for the cook of the Prime Minister, I believe the deluded creature of a husband would have asked Lord John for the loan of him.

IV.

Fitzroy Timmins, whose taste for wine is remarkable for so young a man, is a member of the committee of the "Megatherium Club," and the great Mirobolant, good-natured as all great men are, was only too happy to oblige him. A young friend and protege of his, of considerable merit, M. Cavalcadour, happened to be disengaged through the lamented death of Lord Hauncher, with whom young Cavalcadour had made his debut as an artist. He had nothing to refuse to his master, Mirobolant, and would impress himself to be useful to a gourmet so distinguished as Monsieur Timmins. Fitz went away as pleased as Punch with this encomium of the great Mirobolant, and was one of those who voted against the decreasing of Mirobolant's salary, when the measure was proposed by Mr. Parings, Colonel Close, and the Screw party in the committee of the club.

Faithful to the promise of his great master, the youthful Cavalcadour called in Lilliput Street the next day. A rich crimson velvet waistcoat, with buttons of blue glass and gold, a variegated blue satin stock, over which a graceful mosaic chain hung in glittering folds, a white hat worn on one side of his long curling ringlets, redolent with the most delightful hair-oil--one of those white hats which looks as if it had been just skinned--and a pair of gloves not exactly of the color of beurre frais, but of beurre that has been up the chimney, with a natty cane with a gilt knob, completed the upper part at any rate, of the costume of the young fellow whom the page introduced to Mrs. Timmins.

Her mamma and she had been just having a dispute about the gooseberry-cream when Cavalcadour arrived. His presence silenced Mrs. Gashleigh; and Rosa, in carrying on a conversation with him in the French language, which she had acquired perfectly in an elegant finishing establishment in Kensington Square, had a great advantage over her mother, who could only pursue the dialogue with very much difficulty, eying one or other interlocutor with an alarmed and suspicious look, and gasping out "We" whenever she thought a proper opportunity arose for the use of that affirmative.

"I have two leetl menus weez me," said Cavalcadour to Mrs. Gashleigh.

"Minews, yes, oh, indeed?" answered the lady.

"Two little cartes."

"Oh, two carts! Oh, we," she said. "Coming, I suppose?" And she looked out of the window to see if they were there.

Cavalcadour smiled. He produced from a pocket-book a pink paper and a blue paper, on which he had written two bills of fare, the last two which he had composed for the lamented Hauncher and he handed these over to Mrs. Fitzroy.

The poor little woman was dreadfully puzzled with these documents, (she has them in her possession still,) and began to read from the pink one as follows:--

"DINER POUR 16 PERSONNES.

Potage (clair) a la Rigodon.
Do. a la Prince de Tombuctou.

Deux Poissons.
Rougets Gratines   a la Boadicee.

Saumon de Severne
a la Cleopatre.

Deux Releves.
Le Chapeau-a-trois-cornes farci a la Robespierre.
Le Tire-botte a l'Odalisque.

Six Entrees.
Saute de Hannetons a l'Epingliere.
Cotelettes a la Megatherium.
Bourrasque de Veau a la Palsambleu.
Laitances de Carpe en goguette a la Reine Pomare.
Turban de Volaille a l'Archeveque de Cantorbery."

And so on with the entremets, and hors d'oeuvres, and the rotis, and the releves.

"Madame will see that the dinners are quite simple," said M. Cavalcadour.

"Oh, quite!" said Rosa, dreadfully puzzled.

"Which would Madame like?"

"Which would we like, mamma?" Rosa asked; adding, as if after a little thought, "I think, sir, we should prefer the blue one." At which Mrs. Gashleigh nodded as knowingly as she could; though pink or blue, I defy anybody to know what these cooks mean by their jargon.

"If you please, Madame, we will go down below and examine the scene of operations," Monsieur Cavalcadour said; and so he was marshalled down the stairs to the kitchen, which he didn't like to name, and appeared before the cook in all his splendor.

He cast a rapid glance round the premises, and a smile of something like contempt lighted up his features. "Will you bring pen and ink, if you please, and I will write down a few of the articles which will be necessary for us? We shall require, if you please, eight more stew-pans, a couple of braising-pans, eight saute-pans, six bainmarie-pans, a freezing-pot with accessories, and a few more articles of which I will inscribe the names." And Mr. Cavalcadour did so, dashing down, with the rapidity of genius, a tremendous list of ironmongery goods, which he handed over to Mrs. Timmins. She and her mamma were quite frightened by the awful catalogue.

"I will call three days hence and superintend the progress of matters; and we will make the stock for the soup the day before the dinner."

"Don't you think, sir," here interposed Mrs. Gashleigh, "that one soup, a fine rich mock-turtle, such as I have seen in the best houses in the West of England, and such as the late Lord Fortyskewer"

"You will get what is wanted for the soups, if you please," Mr. Cavalcadour continued, not heeding this interruption, and as bold as a captain on his own quarter-deck: "for the stock of clear soup, you will get a leg of beef, a leg of veal, and a ham."

"We, munseer," said the cook, dropping a terrified curtsy: "a leg of beef, a leg of veal, and a ham."

"You can't serve a leg of veal at a party," said Mrs. Gashleigh; "and a leg of beef is not a company dish."

"Madame, they are to make the stock of the clear soup," Mr. Cavalcadour said. "WHAT!" cried Mrs. Gashleigh; and the cook repeated his former expression.

"Never, whilst I am in this house," cried out Mrs. Gashleigh, indignantly; "never in a Christian ENGLISH household; never shall such sinful waste be permitted by ME. If you wish me to dine, Rosa, you must get a dinner less EXPENSIVE. The Right Honorable Lord Fortyskewer could dine, sir, without these wicked luxuries, and I presume my daughter's guests can."

"Madame is perfectly at liberty to decide," said M. Cavalcadour. "I came to oblige Madame and my good friend Mirobolant, not myself."

"Thank you, sir, I think it WILL be too expensive," Rosa stammered in a great flutter; "but I am very much obliged to you."

"Il n'y a point d'obligation, Madame," said Monsieur Alcide Camille Cavalcadour in his most superb manner; and, making a splendid bow to the lady of the house, was respectfully conducted to the upper regions by little Buttons, leaving Rosa frightened, the cook amazed and silent, and Mrs. Gashleigh boiling with indignation against the dresser.

Up to that moment, Mrs. Blowser, the cook, who had come out of Devonshire with Mrs. Gashleigh (of course that lady garrisoned her daughter's house with servants, and expected them to give her information of everything which took place there) up to that moment, I say, the cook had been quite contented with that subterraneous station which she occupied in life, and had a pride in keeping her kitchen neat, bright, and clean. It was, in her opinion, the comfortablest room in the house (we all thought so when we came down of a night to smoke there), and the handsomest kitchen in Lilliput Street.

But after the visit of Cavalcadour, the cook became quite discontented and uneasy in her mind. She talked in a melancholy manner over the area-railings to the cooks at twenty-three and twenty-five. She stepped over the way, and conferred with the cook there. She made inquiries at the baker's and at other places about the kitchens in the great houses in Brobdingnag Gardens, and how many spits, bangmarry-pans, and stoo-pans they had. She thought she could not do with an occasional help, but must have a kitchen-maid. And she was often discovered by a gentleman of the police force, who was, I believe, her cousin, and occasionally visited her when Mrs. Gashleigh was not in the house or spying it:--she was discovered seated with MRS. RUNDELL in her lap, its leaves bespattered with her tears. "My pease be gone, Pelisse," she said, "zins I zaw that ther Franchman!" And it was all the faithful fellow could do to console her.

"---- the dinner!" said Timmins, in a rage at last. "Having it cooked in the house is out of the question. The bother of it, and the row your mother makes, are enough to drive one mad. It won't happen again, I can promise you, Rosa. Order it at Fubsby's, at once. You can have everything from Fubsby's, from footmen to saltspoons. Let's go and order it at Fubsby's."

"Darling, if you don't mind the expense, and it will be any relief to you, let us do as you wish," Rosa said; and she put on her bonnet, and they went off to the grand cook and confectioner of the Brobdingnag quarter.

V.

On the arm of her Fitzroy, Rosa went off to Fubsby's, that magnificent shop at the corner of Parliament Place and Alicompayne Square, a shop into which the rogue had often cast a glance of approbation as he passed: for there are not only the most wonderful and delicious cakes and confections in the window, but at the counter there are almost sure to be three or four of the prettiest women in the whole of this world, with little darling caps of the last French make, with beautiful wavy hair, and the neatest possible waists and aprons.

Yes, there they sit; and others, perhaps, besides Fitz have cast a sheep's-eye through those enormous plate-glass windowpanes. I suppose it is the fact of perpetually living among such a quantity of good things that makes those young ladies so beautiful. They come into the place, let us say, like ordinary people, and gradually grow handsomer and handsomer, until they grow out into the perfect angels you see. It can't be otherwise: if you and I, my dear fellow, were to have a course of that place, we should become beautiful too. They live in an atmosphere of the most delicious pine-apples, blanc-manges, creams, (some whipt, and some so good that of course they don't want whipping,) jellies, tipsy-cakes, cherry-brandy, one hundred thousand sweet and lovely things. Look at the preserved fruits, look at the golden ginger, the outspreading ananas, the darling little rogues of China oranges, ranged in the gleaming crystal cylinders. Mon Dieu! Look at the strawberries in the leaves. Each of them is as large nearly as a lady's reticule, and looks as if it had been brought up in a nursery to itself. One of those strawberries is a meal for those young ladies, behind the counter; they nibble off a little from the side, and if they are very hungry, which can scarcely ever happen, they are allowed to go to the crystal canisters and take out a rout-cake or macaroon. In the evening they sit and tell each other little riddles out of the bonbons; and when they wish to amuse themselves, they read the most delightful remarks, in the French language, about Love, and Cupid, and Beauty, before they place them inside the crackers. They always are writing down good things into Mr. Fubsby's ledgers. It must be a perfect feast to read them. Talk of the Garden of Eden! I believe it was nothing to Mr. Fubsby's house; and I have no doubt that after those young ladies have been there a certain time, they get to such a pitch of loveliness at last, that they become complete angels, with wings sprouting out of their lovely shoulders, when (after giving just a preparatory balance or two) they fly up to the counter and perch there for a minute, hop down again, and affectionately kiss the other young ladies, and say, "Good-by, dears! We shall meet again la haut." And then with a whir of their deliciously scented wings, away they fly for good, whisking over the trees of Brobdingnag Square, and up into the sky, as the policeman touches his hat.

It is up there that they invent the legends for the crackers, and the wonderful riddles and remarks on the bonbons. No mortal, I am sure, could write them.

I never saw a man in such a state as Fitzroy Timmins in the presence of those ravishing houris. Mrs. Fitz having explained that they required a dinner for twenty persons, the chief young lady asked what Mr. and Mrs. Fitz would like, and named a thousand things, each better than the other, to all of which Fitz instantly said yes. The wretch was in such a state of infatuation that I believe if that lady had proposed to him a fricasseed elephant, or a boa-constrictor in jelly, he would have said, "O yes, certainly; put it down."

That Peri wrote down in her album a list of things which it would make your mouth water to listen to. But she took it all quite calmly. Heaven bless you! THEY don't care about things that are no delicacies to them! But whatever she chose to write down, Fitzroy let her.

After the dinner and dessert were ordered (at Fubsby's they furnish everything: dinner and dessert, plate and china, servants in your own livery, and, if you please, guests of title too), the married couple retreated from that shop of wonders; Rosa delighted that the trouble of the dinner was all off their hands but she was afraid it would be rather expensive.

"Nothing can be too expensive which pleases YOU, dear," Fitz said.
"By the way, one of those young women was rather good-looking," Rosa remarked: "the one in the cap with the blue ribbons." (And she cast about the shape of the cap in her mind, and determined to have exactly such another.)

"Think so? I didn't observe," said the miserable hypocrite by her side; and when he had seen Rosa home, he went back, like an infamous fiend, to order something else which he had forgotten, he said, at Fubsby's. Get out of that Paradise, you cowardly, creeping, vile serpent you!

Until the day of the dinner, the infatuated fop was ALWAYS going to Fubsby's. HE WAS REMARKED THERE. He used to go before he went to chambers in the morning, and sometimes on his return from the Temple: but the morning was the time which he preferred; and one day, when he went on one of his eternal pretexts, and was chattering and flirting at the counter, a lady who had been reading yesterday's paper and eating a halfpenny bun for an hour in the back shop (if that paradise may be called a shop) a lady stepped forward, laid down the Morning Herald, and confronted him.

That lady was Mrs. Gashleigh. From that day the miserable Fitzroy was in her power; and she resumed a sway over his house, to shake off which had been the object of his life, and the result of many battles. And for a mere freak (for, on going into Fubsby's a week afterwards he found the Peris drinking tea out of blue cups, and eating stale bread and butter, when his absurd passion instantly vanished) I say, for a mere freak, the most intolerable burden of his life was put on his shoulders again, his mother-in-law.

On the day before the little dinner took place and I promise you we shall come to it in the very next chapter, a tall and elegant middle-aged gentleman, who might have passed for an earl but that there was a slight incompleteness about his hands and feet, the former being uncommonly red, and the latter large and irregular, was introduced to Mrs. Timmins by the page, who announced him as Mr. Truncheon.

"I'm Truncheon, Ma'am," he said, with a low bow.

"Indeed!" said Rosa.

"About the dinner M'm, from Fubsby's, M'm. As you have no butler, M'm, I presume you will wish me to act as sich. I shall bring two persons as haids to-morrow; both answers to the name of John. I'd best, if you please, inspect the premisis, and will think you to allow your young man to show me the pantry and kitching."

Truncheon spoke in a low voice, and with the deepest and most respectful melancholy. There is not much expression in his eyes, but from what there is, you would fancy that he was oppressed by a secret sorrow. Rosa trembled as she surveyed this gentleman's size, his splendid appearance, and gravity. "I am sure," she said, "I never shall dare to ask him to hand a glass of water." Even Mrs. Gashleigh, when she came on the morning of the actual dinner-party, to superintend matters, was cowed, and retreated from the kitchen before the calm majesty of Truncheon.

And yet that great man was, like all the truly great--affable.

He put aside his coat and waistcoat (both of evening cut, and looking prematurely splendid as he walked the streets in noonday), and did not disdain to rub the glasses and polish the decanters, and to show young Buttons the proper mode of preparing these articles for a dinner. And while he operated, the maids, and Buttons, and cook, when she could and what had she but the vegetables to boil? crowded round him, and listened with wonder as he talked of the great families as he had lived with. That man, as they saw him there before them, had been cab-boy to Lord Tantallan, valet to the Earl of Bareacres, and groom of the chambers to the Duchess Dowager of Fitzbattleaxe. Oh, it was delightful to hear Mr. Truncheon!

VI.

On the great, momentous, stupendous day of the dinner, my beloved female reader may imagine that Fitzroy Timmins was sent about his business at an early hour in the morning, while the women began to make preparations to receive their guests. "There will be no need of your going to Fubsby's," Mrs. Gashleigh said to him, with a look that drove him out of doors. "Everything that we require has been ordered THERE! You will please to be back here at six o'clock, and not sooner: and I presume you will acquiesce in my arrangements about the WINE?"

"O yes, mamma," said the prostrate son-in-law.

"In so large a party--a party beyond some folks MEANS--expensive WINES are ABSURD. The light sherry at 26s., the champagne at 42s.; and you are not to go beyond 36s. for the claret and port after dinner. Mind, coffee will be served; and you come up stairs after two rounds of the claret."

"Of course, of course," acquiesced the wretch; and hurried out of the house to his chambers, and to discharge the commissions with which the womankind had intrusted him.

As for Mrs. Gashleigh, you might have heard her bawling over the house the whole day long. That admirable woman was everywhere: in the kitchen until the arrival of Truncheon, before whom she would not retreat without a battle; on the stairs; in Fitzroy's dressing-room; and in Fitzroy minor's nursery, to whom she gave a dose of her own composition, while the nurse was sent out on a pretext to make purchases of garnish for the dishes to be served for the little dinner. Garnish for the dishes! As if the folks at Fubsby's could not garnish dishes better than Gashleigh, with her stupid old-world devices of laurel-leaves, parsley, and cut turnips! Why, there was not a dish served that day that was not covered over with skewers, on which truffles, crayfish, mushrooms, and forced-meat were impaled. When old Gashleigh went down with her barbarian bunches of holly and greens to stick about the meats, even the cook saw their incongruity, and, at Truncheon's orders, flung the whole shrubbery into the dust-house, where, while poking about the premises, you may be sure Mrs. G. saw it.

Every candle which was to be burned that night (including the tallow candle, which she said was a good enough bed-light for Fitzroy) she stuck into the candlesticks with her own hands, giving her own high-shouldered plated candlesticks of the year 1798 the place of honor. She upset all poor Rosa's floral arrangements, turning the nosegays from one vase into the other without any pity, and was never tired of beating, and pushing, and patting, and WHAPPING the curtain and sofa draperies into shape in the little drawing-room.

In Fitz's own apartments she revelled with peculiar pleasure. It has been described how she had sacked his study and pushed away his papers, some of which, including three cigars, and the commencement of an article for the Law Magazine, "Lives of the Sheriffs' Officers," he has never been able to find to this day. Mamma now went into the little room in the back regions, which is Fitz's dressing-room, (and was destined to be a cloak-room,) and here she rummaged to her heart's delight.

In an incredibly short space of time she examined all his outlying pockets, drawers, and letters; she inspected his socks and handkerchiefs in the top drawers; and on the dressing-table, his razors, shaving-strop, and hair-oil. She carried off his silver-topped scent-bottle out of his dressing-case, and a half-dozen of his favorite pills (which Fitz possesses in common with every well-regulated man), and probably administered them to her own family. His boots, glossy pumps, and slippers she pushed into the shower-bath, where the poor fellow stepped into them the next morning, in the midst of a pool in which they were lying. The baby was found sucking his boot-hooks the next day in the nursery; and as for the bottle of varnish for his shoes, (which he generally paints upon the trees himself, having a pretty taste in that way,) it could never be found to the present hour but it was remarked that the young Master Gashleighs, when they came home for the holidays, always wore lacquered highlows; and the reader may draw his conclusions from THAT fact.

In the course of the day all the servants gave Mrs. Timmins warning.

The cook said she coodn't abear it no longer, 'aving Mrs. G. always about her kitching, with her fingers in all the saucepans. Mrs. G. had got her the place, but she preferred one as Mrs. G. didn't get for her.

The nurse said she was come to nuss Master Fitzroy, and knew her duty; his grandmamma wasn't his nuss, and was always aggrawating her, missus must shoot herself elsewhere.

The housemaid gave utterance to the same sentiments in language more violent.

Little Buttons bounced up to his mistress, said he was butler of the family, Mrs. G. was always poking about his pantry, and dam if he'd stand it.

At every moment Rosa grew more and more bewildered. The baby howled a great deal during the day. His large china christening-bowl was cracked by Mrs. Gashleigh altering the flowers in it, and pretending to be very cool, whilst her hands shook with rage.

"Pray go on, mamma," Rosa said with tears in her eyes. "Should you like to break the chandelier?"

"Ungrateful, unnatural child!" bellowed the other. "Only that I know you couldn't do without me, I'd leave the house this minute."

"As you wish," said Rosa; but Mrs. G. DIDN'T wish: and in this juncture Truncheon arrived.

That officer surveyed the dining-room, laid the cloth there with admirable precision and neatness; ranged the plate on the sideboard with graceful accuracy, but objected to that old thing in the centre, as he called Mrs. Gashleigh's silver basket, as cumbrous and useless for the table, where they would want all the room they could get.

Order was not restored to the house, nor, indeed, any decent progress made, until this great man came: but where there was a revolt before, and a general disposition to strike work and to yell out defiance against Mrs. Gashleigh, who was sitting bewildered and furious in the drawing-room--where there was before commotion, at the appearance of the master-spirit, all was peace and unanimity: the cook went back to her pans, the housemaid busied herself with the china and glass, cleaning some articles and breaking others, Buttons sprang up and down the stairs, obedient to the orders of his chief, and all things went well and in their season.

At six, the man with the wine came from Binney and Latham's. At a quarter past six, Timmins himself arrived.

At half past six he might have been heard shouting out for his varnished boots but we know where THOSE had been hidden and for his dressing things; but Mrs. Gashleigh had put them away.

As in his vain inquiries for these articles he stood shouting, "Nurse! Buttons! Rosa my dear!" and the most fearful execrations up and down the stairs, Mr. Truncheon came out on him.

"Egscuse me, sir," says he, "but it's impawsable. We can't dine twenty at that table--not if you set 'em out awinder, we can't."

"What's to be done?" asked Fitzroy, in an agony; "they've all said they'd come."

"Can't do it," said the other; "with two top and bottom and your table is as narrow as a bench, we can't hold more than heighteen, and then each person's helbows will be into his neighbor's cheer."

"Rosa! Mrs. Gashleigh!" cried out Timmins, "come down and speak to this gentl--this-"

"Truncheon, sir," said the man.

The women descended from the drawing-room. "Look and see, ladies," he said, inducting them into the dining-room: "there's the room, there's the table laid for heighteen, and I defy you to squeege in more."

"One person in a party always fails," said Mrs. Gashleigh, getting alarmed. "That's nineteen," Mr. Truncheon remarked. "We must knock another hoff, Ma'm." And he looked her hard in the face.

Mrs. Gashleigh was very red and nervous, and paced, or rather squeezed round the table (it was as much as she could do). The chairs could not be put any closer than they were. It was impossible, unless the convive sat as a centre-piece in the middle, to put another guest at that table.

"Look at that lady movin' round, sir. You see now the difficklty. If my men wasn't thinner, they couldn't hoperate at all," Mr. Truncheon observed, who seemed to have a spite to Mrs. Gashleigh.

"What is to be done?" she said, with purple accents.

"My dearest mamma," Rosa cried out, "you must stop at home, how sorry I am!"

And she shot one glance at Fitzroy, who shot another at the great Truncheon, who held down his eyes. "We could manage with heighteen," he said, mildly.

Mrs. Gashleigh gave a hideous laugh.

She went away. At eight o'clock she was pacing at the corner of the street, and actually saw the company arrive. First came the Topham Sawyers, in their light-blue carriage with the white hammercloth and blue and white ribbons, their footmen drove the house down with the knocking.

Then followed the ponderous and snuff-colored vehicle, with faded gilt wheels and brass earl's coronets all over it, the conveyance of the House of Bungay. The Countess of Bungay and daughter stepped out of the carriage. The fourteenth Earl of Bungay couldn't come.

Sir Thomas and Lady Gulpin's fly made its appearance, from which issued the General with his star, and Lady Gulpin in yellow satin. The Rowdys' brougham followed next; after which Mrs. Butt's handsome equipage drove up.

The two friends of the house, young gentlemen from the Temple, now arrived in cab No. 9996. We tossed up, in fact, which should pay the fare.

Mr. Ranville Ranville walked, and was dusting his boots as the Templars drove up. Lord Castlemouldy came out of a twopenny omnibus. Funnyman, the wag, came last, whirling up rapidly in a hansom, just as Mrs. Gashleigh, with rage in her heart, was counting that two people had failed, and that there were only seventeen after all.

Mr. Truncheon passed our names to Mr. Billiter, who bawled them out on the stairs. Rosa was smiling in a pink dress, and looking as fresh as an angel, and received her company with that grace which has always characterized her.

The moment of the dinner arrived, old Lady Bungay scuffled off on the arm of Fitzroy, while the rear was brought up by Rosa and Lord Castlemouldy, of Ballyshanvanvoght Castle, co, Tipperary. Some fellows who had the luck took down ladies to dinner. I was not sorry to be out of the way of Mrs. Rowdy, with her dandified airs, or of that high and mighty county princess, Mrs. Topham Sawyer.

VII.

Of course it does not become the present writer, who has partaken of the best entertainment which his friends could supply, to make fun of their (somewhat ostentatious, as it must be confessed) hospitality.

If they gave a dinner beyond their means, it is no business of mine. I hate a man who goes and eats a friend's meat, and then blabs the secrets of the mahogany. Such a man deserves never to be asked to dinner again; and though at the close of a London season that seems no great loss, and you sicken of a whitebait as you would of a whale yet we must always remember that there's another season coming, and hold our tongues for the present.

As for describing, then, the mere victuals on Timmins's table, that would be absurd. Everybody (I mean of the genteel world of course, of which I make no doubt the reader is a polite ornament) Everybody has the same everything in London. You see the same coats, the same dinners, the same boiled fowls and mutton, the same cutlets, fish, and cucumbers, the same lumps of Wenham Lake ice, &c. The waiters with white neck-cloths are as like each other everywhere as the peas which they hand round with the ducks of the second course. Can't any one invent anything new?

The only difference between Timmins's dinner and his neighbor's was, that he had hired, as we have said, the greater part of the plate, and that his cowardly conscience magnified faults and disasters of which no one else probably took heed.

But Rosa thought, from the supercilious air with which Mrs. Topham Sawyer was eying the plate and other arrangements, that she was remarking the difference of the ciphers on the forks and spoons--which had, in fact, been borrowed from every one of Fitzroy's friends--(I know, for instance, that he had my six, among others, and only returned five, along with a battered old black-pronged plated abomination, which I have no doubt belongs to Mrs. Gashleigh, whom I hereby request to send back mine in exchange) their guilty consciences, I say, made them fancy that everyone was spying out their domestic deficiencies: whereas, it is probable that nobody present thought of their failings at all. People never do: they never see holes in their neighbors' coats, they are too indolent, simple, and charitable.

Some things, however, one could not help remarking: for instance, though Fitz is my closest friend, yet could I avoid seeing and being amused by his perplexity and his dismal efforts to be facetious? His eye wandered all round the little room with quick uneasy glances, very different from those frank and jovial looks with which he is accustomed to welcome you to a leg of mutton; and Rosa, from the other end of the table, and over the flowers, entree dishes, and wine-coolers, telegraphed him with signals of corresponding alarm. Poor devils! why did they ever go beyond that leg of mutton?

Funnyman was not brilliant in conversation, scarcely opening his mouth, except for the purposes of feasting. The fact is, our friend Tom Dawson was at table, who knew all his stories, and in his presence the greatest wag is always silent and uneasy.

Fitz has a very pretty wit of his own, and a good reputation on circuit; but he is timid before great people. And indeed the presence of that awful Lady Bungay on his right hand was enough to damp him. She was in court mourning (for the late Prince of Schlippenschloppen). She had on a large black funereal turban and appurtenances, and a vast breastplate of twinkling, twiddling black bugles. No wonder a man could not be gay in talking to HER.

Mrs. Rowdy and Mrs. Topham Sawyer love each other as women do who have the same receiving nights, and ask the same society; they were only separated by Ranville Ranville, who tries to be well with both and they talked at each other across him.

Topham and Rowdy growled out a conversation about Rum, Ireland, and the Navigation Laws, quite unfit for print. Sawyer never speaks three words without mentioning the House and the Speaker.

The Irish Peer said nothing (which was a comfort) but he ate and drank of everything which came in his way; and cut his usual absurd figure in dyed whiskers and a yellow under-waistcoat.

General Gulpin sported his star, and looked fat and florid, but melancholy. His wife ordered away his dinner, just like honest Sancho's physician at Barataria.

Botherby's stories about Lamartine are as old as the hills, since the barricades of 1848; and he could not get in a word or cut the slightest figure. And as for Tom Dawson, he was carrying on an undertoned small-talk with Lady Barbara St. Mary's, so that there was not much conversation worth record going on WITHIN the dining-room.

Outside it was different. Those houses in Lilliput Street are so uncommonly compact, that you can hear everything which takes place all over the tenement; and so-

In the awful pauses of the banquet, and the hall-door being furthermore open, we had the benefit of hearing:

The cook, and the occasional cook, below stairs, exchanging rapid phrases regarding the dinner;

The smash of the soup-tureen, and swift descent of the kitchen-maid and soup-ladle down the stairs to the lower regions. This accident created a laugh, and rather amused Fitzroy and the company, and caused Funnyman to say, bowing to Rosa, that she was mistress of herself, though China fall. But she did not heed him, for at that moment another noise commenced, namely, that of-

The baby in the upper rooms, who commenced a series of piercing yells, which, though stopped by the sudden clapping to of the nursery-door, were only more dreadful to the mother when suppressed. She would have given a guinea to go up stairs and have done with the whole entertainment.

A thundering knock came at the door very early after the dessert, and the poor soul took a speedy opportunity of summoning the ladies to depart, though you may be sure it was only old Mrs. Gashleigh, who had come with her daughters, of course the first person to come. I saw her red gown whisking up the stairs, which were covered with plates and dishes, over which she trampled.

Instead of having any quiet after the retreat of the ladies, the house was kept in a rattle, and the glasses jingled on the table as the flymen and coachmen plied the knocker, and the soiree came in.

From my place I could see everything: the guests as they arrived (I remarked very few carriages, mostly cabs and flies), and a little crowd of blackguard boys and children, who were formed round the door, and gave ironical cheers to the folks as they stepped out of their vehicles.

As for the evening-party, if a crowd in the dog-days is pleasant, poor Mrs. Timmins certainly had a successful soiree. You could hardly move on the stair.

Mrs. Sternhold broke in the banisters, and nearly fell through. There was such a noise and chatter you could not hear the singing of the Miss Gashleighs, which was no great loss. Lady Bungay could hardly get to her carriage, being entangled with Colonel Wedgewood in the passage. An absurd attempt was made to get up a dance of some kind; but before Mrs. Crowder had got round the room, the hanging-lamp in the dining-room below was stove in, and fell with a crash on the table, now prepared for refreshment.

Why, in fact, did the Timminses give that party at all? It was quite beyond their means. They have offended a score of their old friends, and pleased none of their acquaintances. So angry were many who were not asked, that poor Rosa says she must now give a couple more parties and take in those not previously invited. And I know for a fact that Fubsby's bill is not yet paid; nor Binney and Latham's the wine-merchants; that the breakage and hire of glass and china cost ever so much money; that every true friend of Timmins has cried out against his absurd extravagance, and that now, when every one is going out of town, Fitz has hardly money to pay his circuit, much more to take Rosa to a watering-place, as he wished and promised.

As for Mrs. Gashleigh, the only feasible plan of economy which she can suggest, is that she could come and live with her daughter and son-in-law, and that they should keep house together. If he agrees to this, she has a little sum at the banker's, with which she would not mind easing his present difficulties; and the poor wretch is so utterly bewildered and crestfallen that it is very likely he will become her victim.

The Topham Sawyers, when they go down into the country, will represent Fitz as a ruined man and reckless prodigal; his uncle, the attorney, from whom he has expectations, will most likely withdraw his business, and adopt some other member of his family--Blanche Crowder for instance, whose husband, the doctor, has had high words with poor Fitzroy already, of course at the women's instigation. And all these accumulated miseries fall upon the unfortunate wretch because he was good-natured, and his wife would have a Little Dinner.

Mrs. Perkins's Ball

THE MULLIGAN (OF BALLYMULLIGAN), AND HOW WE WENT TO MRS. PERKINS'S BALL.

I do not know where Ballymulligan is, and never knew anybody who did. Once I asked the Mulligan the question, when that chieftain assumed a look of dignity so ferocious, and spoke of "Saxon curiawsitee" in a tone of such evident displeasure, that, as after all it can matter very little to me whereabouts lies the Celtic principality in question, I have never pressed the inquiry any farther.

I don't know even the Mulligan's town residence. One night, as he bade us adieu in Oxford Street, "I live THERE," says he, pointing down towards Oxbridge, with the big stick he carries, so his abode is in that direction at any rate. He has his letters addressed to several of his friends' houses, and his parcels, &c. are left for him at various taverns which he frequents. That pair of checked trousers, in which you see him attired, he did me the favor of ordering from my own tailor, who is quite as anxious as anybody to know the address of the wearer. In like manner my hatter asked me, "Oo was the Hirish gent as 'ad ordered four 'ats and a sable boar to be sent to my lodgings?" As I did not know (however I might guess) the articles have never been sent, and the Mulligan has withdrawn his custom from the "infernal four-and-nine-penny scoundthrel," as he calls him. The hatter has not shut up shop in consequence.

I became acquainted with the Mulligan through a distinguished countryman of his, who, strange to say, did not know the chieftain himself. But dining with my friend Fred Clancy, of the Irish bar, at Greenwich, the Mulligan came up, "inthrojuiced" himself to Clancy as he said, claimed relationship with him on the side of Brian Boroo, and drawing his chair to our table, quickly became intimate with us. He took a great liking to me, was good enough to find out my address and pay me a visit: since which period often and often on coming to breakfast in the morning I have found him in my sitting-room on the sofa engaged with the rolls and morning papers: and many a time, on returning home at night for an evening's quiet reading, I have discovered this honest fellow in the arm-chair before the fire, perfuming the apartment with my cigars and trying the quality of such liquors as might be found on the sideboard. The way in which he pokes fun at Betsy, the maid of the lodgings, is prodigious. She begins to laugh whenever he comes; if he calls her a duck, a divvle, a darlin', it is all one. He is just as much a master of the premises as the individual who rents them at fifteen shillings a week; and as for handkerchiefs, shirt-collars, and the like articles of fugitive haberdashery, the loss since I have known him is unaccountable. I suspect he is like the cat in some houses: for, suppose the whiskey, the cigars, the sugar, the tea-caddy, the pickles, and other groceries disappear, all is laid upon that edax-rerum of a Mulligan.

The greatest offence that can be offered to him is to call him MR. Mulligan. "Would you deprive me, sir," says he, "of the title which was bawrun be me princelee ancestors in a hundred thousand battles? In our own green valleys and fawrests, in the American savannahs, in the sierras of Speen and the flats of Flandthers, the Saxon has quailed before me war-cry of MULLIGAN ABOO! MR. Mulligan! I'll pitch anybody out of the window who calls me MR. Mulligan." He said this, and uttered the slogan of the Mulligans with a shriek so terrific, that my uncle (the Rev. W. Gruels, of the Independent Congregation, Bungay), who had happened to address him in the above obnoxious manner, while sitting at my apartments drinking tea after the May meetings, instantly quitted the room, and has never taken the least notice of me since, except to state to the rest of the family that I am doomed irrevocably to perdition.

Well, one day last season, I had received from my kind and most estimable friend, MRS. PERKINS OF POCKLINGTON SQUARE (to whose amiable family I have had the honor of giving lessons in drawing, French, and the German flute), an invitation couched in the usual terms, on satin gilt-edged note-paper, to her evening-party; or, as I call it, "Ball."

Besides the engraved note sent to all her friends, my kind patroness had addressed me privately as follows:-

MY DEAR MR. TITMARSH, If you know any VERY eligible young man, we give you leave to bring him. You GENTLEMEN love your CLUBS so much now, and care so little for DANCING, that it is really quite A SCANDAL. Come early, and before EVERYBODY, and give us the benefit of all your taste and CONTINENTAL SKILL. "Your sincere "EMILY PERKINS."

"Whom shall I bring?" mused I, highly flattered by this mark of confidence; and I thought of Bob Trippett; and little Fred Spring, of the Navy Pay Office; Hulker, who is rich, and I knew took lessons in Paris; and a half-score of other bachelor friends, who might be considered as VERY ELIGIBLE--when I was roused from my meditation by the slap of a hand on my shoulder; and looking up, there was the Mulligan, who began, as usual, reading the papers on my desk.

"Hwhat's this?" says he. "Who's Perkins? Is it a supper-ball, or only a tay-ball?"

"The Perkinses of Pocklington Square, Mulligan, are tiptop people," says I, with a tone of dignity. "Mr. Perkins's sister is married to a baronet, Sir Giles Bacon, of Hogwash, Norfolk. Mr. Perkins's uncle was Lord Mayor of London; and he was himself in Parliament, and MAY BE again any day. The family are my most particular friends. A tay-ball indeed! why, Gunter . . ." Here I stopped: I felt I was committing myself.

"Gunter!" says the Mulligan, with another confounded slap on the shoulder. "Don't say another word: I'LL go widg you, my boy."

"YOU go, Mulligan?" says I: "why, really- I - it's not my party."

"Your hwhawt? hwhat's this letter? a'n't I an eligible young man? Is the descendant of a thousand kings unfit company for a miserable tallow-chandthlering cockney? Are ye joking wid me? for, let me tell ye, I don't like them jokes. D'ye suppose I'm not as well bawrun and bred as yourself, or any Saxon friend ye ever had?"

"I never said you weren't, Mulligan," says I.

"Ye don't mean seriously that a Mulligan is not fit company for a Perkins?"

"My dear fellow, how could you think I could so far insult you?" says I. "Well, then," says he, "that's a matter settled, and we go."

What the deuce was I to do? I wrote to Mrs. Perkins; and that kind lady replied, that she would receive the Mulligan, or any other of my friends, with the greatest cordiality. "Fancy a party, all Mulligans!" thought I, with a secret terror.

MR. AND MRS. PERKINS, THEIR HOUSE, AND THEIR YOUNG PEOPLE.

Following Mrs. Perkins's orders, the present writer made his appearance very early at Pocklington Square: where the tastiness of all the decorations elicited my warmest admiration. Supper of course was in the dining-loom, superbly arranged by Messrs. Grigs and Spooner, the confectioners of the neighborhood. I assisted my respected friend Mr. Perkins and his butler in decanting the sherry, and saw, not without satisfaction, a large bath for wine under the sideboard, in which were already placed very many bottles of champagne.

The BACK DINING-ROOM, Mr. P.'s study (where the venerable man goes to sleep after dinner), was arranged on this occasion as a tea-room, Mrs. Flouncey (Miss Fanny's maid) officiating in a cap and pink ribbons, which became her exceedingly. Long, long before the arrival of the company, I remarked Master Thomas Perkins and Master Giles Bacon, his cousin (son of Sir Giles Bacon, Bart.), in this apartment, busy among the macaroons.

Mr. Gregory the butler, besides John the footman and Sir Giles's large man in the Bacon livery, and honest Grundsell, carpet-beater and green-grocer, of Little Pocklington Buildings, had at least half a dozen of aides-de-camp in black with white neck-cloths, like doctors of divinity.

The BACK DRAWING-ROOM door on the landing being taken off the hinges (and placed up stairs under Mr. Perkins's bed), the orifice was covered with muslin, and festooned with elegant wreaths of flowers. This was the Dancing Saloon. A linen was spread over the carpet; and a band, consisting of Mr. Clapperton, piano, Mr. Pinch, harp, and Herr Spoff, cornet-a-piston arrived at a pretty early hour, and were accommodated with some comfortable negus in the tea-room, previous to the commencement of their delightful labors. The boudoir to the left was fitted up as a card-room; the drawing-room was of course for the reception of the company, the chandeliers and yellow damask being displayed this night in all their splendor; and the charming conservatory over the landing was ornamented by a few moon-like lamps, and the flowers arranged so that it had the appearance of a fairy bower. And Miss Perkins (as I took the liberty of stating to her mamma) looked like the fairy of that bower. It is this young creature's first year in PUBLIC LIFE: she has been educated, regardless of expense, at Hammersmith; and a simple white muslin dress and blue ceinture set off charms of which I beg to speak with respectful admiration.

My distinguished friend the Mulligan of Ballymulligan was good enough to come the very first of the party. By the way, how awkward it is to be the first of the party! and yet you know somebody must; but for my part, being timid, I always wait at the corner of the street in the cab, and watch until some other carriage comes up.

Well, as we were arranging the sherry in the decanters down the supper-tables, my friend arrived: "Hwhares me friend Mr. Titmarsh?" I heard him bawling out to Gregory in the passage, and presently he rushed into the supper-room, where Mr. and Mrs. Perkins and myself were, and as the waiter was announcing "Mr. Mulligan," "THE Mulligan of Ballymulligan, ye blackguard!" roared he, and stalked into the apartment, "apologoizing," as he said, for introducing himself.

Mr. and Mrs. Perkins did not perhaps wish to be seen in this room, which was for the present only lighted by a couple of candles; but HE was not at all abashed by the circumstance, and grasping them both warmly by the hands, he instantly made himself at home. "As friends of my dear and talented friend Mick," so he is pleased to call me, "I'm deloighted, madam, to be made known to ye. Don't consider me in the light of a mere acquaintance! As for you, my dear madam, you put me so much in moind of my own blessed mother, now resoiding at Ballymulligan Castle, that I begin to love ye at first soight." At which speech Mr. Perkins getting rather alarmed, asked the Mulligan whether he would take some wine, or go up stairs.

"Faix," says Mulligan "it's never too soon for good dhrink." And (although he smelt very much of whiskey already) he drank a tumbler of wine "to the improvement of an acqueentence which comminces in a manner so deloightful."

"Let's go up stairs, Mulligan," says I, and led the noble Irishman to the upper apartments, which were in a profound gloom, the candles not being yet illuminated, and where we surprised Miss Fanny, seated in the twilight at the piano, timidly trying the tunes of the polka which she danced so exquisitely that evening. She did not perceive the stranger at first; but how she started when the Mulligan loomed upon her.

"Heavenlee enchanthress!" says Mulligan, "don't floy at the approach of the humblest of your sleeves! Reshewm your pleece at that insthrument, which weeps harmonious, or smoils melojious, as you charrum it!

Are you acqueented with the Oirish Melodies? Can ye play, 'Who fears to talk of Nointy-eight?' the 'Shan Van Voght?' or the 'Dirge of Ollam Fodhlah?'"

"Who's this mad chap that Titmarsh has brought?" I heard Master Bacon exclaim to Master Perkins. "Look! how frightened Fanny looks!"

"O poo! gals are ALWAYS frightened," Fanny's brother replied; but Giles Bacon, more violent, said, "I'll tell you what, Tom: if this goes on, we must pitch into him." And so I have no doubt they would, when another thundering knock coming, Gregory rushed into the room and began lighting all the candles, so as to produce an amazing brilliancy, Miss Fanny sprang up and ran to her mamma, and the young gentlemen slid down the banisters to receive the company in the hall.

EVERYBODY BEGINS TO COME, BUT ESPECIALLY MR. MINCHIN.

"It's only me and my sisters," Master Bacon said; though "only" meant eight in this instance. All the young ladies had fresh cheeks and purple elbows; all had white frocks, with hair more or less auburn: and so a party was already made of this blooming and numerous family, before the rest of the company began to arrive. The three Miss Meggots next came in their fly: Mr. Blades and his niece from 19 in the square: Captain and Mrs. Struther, and Miss Struther: Doctor Toddy's two daughters and their mamma: but where were the gentlemen? The Mulligan, great and active as he was, could not suffice among so many beauties. At last came a brisk neat little knock, and looking into the hall, I saw a gentleman taking off his clogs there, whilst Sir Giles Bacon's big footman was looking on with rather a contemptuous air.

"What name shall I enounce?" says he, with a wink at Gregory on the stair.

The gentleman in clogs said, with quiet dignity,--

MR. FREDERICK MINCHIN.

"Pump Court, Temple," is printed on his cards in very small type: and he is a rising barrister of the Western Circuit. He is to be found at home of mornings: afterwards "at Westminster," as you read on his back door. "Binks and Minchin's Reports" are probably known to my legal friends: this is the Minchin in question.

He is decidedly genteel, and is rather in request at the balls of the Judges' and Serjeants' ladies: for he dances irreproachably, and goes out to dinner as much as ever he can.

He mostly dines at the Oxford and Cambridge Club, of which you can easily see by his appearance that he is a member; he takes the joint and his half-pint of wine, for Minchin does everything like a gentleman. He is rather of a literary turn; still makes Latin verses with some neatness; and before he was called, was remarkably fond of the flute.

When Mr. Minchin goes out in the evening, his clerk brings his bag to the Club, to dress; and if it is at all muddy, he turns up his trousers, so that he may come in without a speck. For such a party as this, he will have new gloves; otherwise Frederick, his clerk, is chiefly employed in cleaning them with India-rubber.

He has a number of pleasant stories about the Circuit and the University, which he tells with a simper to his neighbor at dinner; and has always the last joke of Mr. Baron Maule. He has a private fortune of five thousand pounds; he is a dutiful son; he has a sister married, in Harley Street; and Lady Jane Ranville has the best opinion of him, and says he is a most excellent and highly principled young man.

Her ladyship and daughter arrived just as Mr. Minchin had popped his clogs into the umbrella-stand; and the rank of that respected person, and the dignified manner in which he led her up stairs, caused all sneering on the part of the domestics to disappear.

THE BALL-ROOM DOOR.

A hundred of knocks follow Frederick Minchin's: in half an hour Messrs. Spoff, Pinch, and Clapperton have begun their music, and Mulligan, with one of the Miss Bacons, is dancing majestically in the first quadrille. My young friends Giles and Tom prefer the landing-place to the drawing-rooms, where they stop all night, robbing the refreshment-trays as they come up or down. Giles has eaten fourteen ices: he will have a dreadful stomach-ache to-morrow. Tom has eaten twelve, but he has had four more glasses of negus than Giles. Grundsell, the occasional waiter, from whom Master Tom buys quantities of ginger-beer, can of course deny him nothing. That is Grundsell, in the tights, with the tray. Meanwhile direct your attention to the three gentlemen at the door: they are conversing.

1st Gent. Who's the man of the house, the bald man?

2nd Gent. Of course. The man of the house is always bald. He's a stockbroker, I believe. Snooks brought me.

1st Gent. Have you been to the tea-room? There's a pretty girl in the tea-room; blue eyes, pink ribbons, that kind of thing.

2nd Gent. Who the deuce is that girl with those tremendous shoulders? Gad! I do wish somebody would smack 'em.

3rd Gent. Sir, that young lady is my niece, sir, my niece, my name is Blades, sir.

2nd Gent. Well, Blades! smack your niece's shoulders: she deserves it, begad! she does. Come in, Jinks, present me to the Perkinses. Hullo! here's an old country acquaintance--Lady Bacon, as I live! with all the piglings; she never goes out without the whole litter. (Exeunt 1st and 2nd Gents.)

LADY BACON, THE MISS BACONS, MR. FLAM.

Lady B. Leonora! Maria! Amelia! here is the gentleman we met at Sir John Porkington's.

[The MISSES BACON, expecting to be asked to dance, smile simultaneously, and begin to smooth their tuckers.]

Mr. Flam. Lady Bacon! I couldn't be mistaken in YOU! Won't you dance, Lady Bacon?

Lady B. Go away, you droll creature!

Mr. Flam. And these are your ladyship's seven lovely sisters, to judge from their likenesses to the charming Lady Bacon?

Lady B. My sisters, he! he! my DAUGHTERS, Mr. Flam, and THEY dance, don't you, girls?

The Misses Bacon. O yes!

Mr. Flam. Gad! how I wish I was a dancing man!

[Exit FLAM.

MR. LARKINS.

I have not been able to do justice (only a Lawrence could do that) to my respected friend Mrs. Perkins, in this picture; but Larkins's portrait is considered very like. Adolphus Larkins has been long connected with Mr. Perkins's City establishment, and is asked to dine twice or thrice per annum. Evening-parties are the great enjoyment of this simple youth, who, after he has walked from Kentish Town to Thames Street, and passed twelve hours in severe labor there, and walked back again to Kentish Town, finds no greater pleasure than to attire his lean person in that elegant evening costume which you see, to walk into town again, and to dance at anybody's house who will invite him. Islington, Pentonville, Somers Town, are the scenes of many of his exploits; and I have seen this good-natured fellow performing figure-dances at Notting-hill, at a house where I am ashamed to say there was no supper, no negus even to speak of, nothing but the bare merits of the polka in which Adolphus revels. To describe this gentleman's infatuation for dancing, let me say, in a word, that he will even frequent boarding-house hops, rather than not go.

He has clogs, too, like Minchin: but nobody laughs at HIM. He gives himself no airs; but walks into a house with a knock and a demeanor so tremulous and humble, that the servants rather patronize him. He does not speak, or have any particular opinions, but when the time comes, begins to dance. He bleats out a word or two to his partner during this operation, seems very weak and sad during the whole performance, and, of course, is set to dance with the ugliest women everywhere.

The gentle, kind spirit! when I think of him night after night, hopping and jigging, and trudging off to Kentish Town, so gently, through the fogs, and mud, and darkness: I do not know whether I ought to admire him, because his enjoyments are so simple, and his dispositions so kindly; or laugh at him, because he draws his life so exquisitely mild. Well, well, we can't be all roaring lions in this world; there must be SOME lambs, and harmless, kindly, gregarious creatures for eating and shearing. See! even good-natured Mrs. Perkins is leading up the trembling Larkins to the tremendous Miss Bunion!

MISS BUNION.

The Poetess, author of "Heartstrings," "The Deadly Nightshade," "Passion Flowers," &c. Though her poems breathe only of love, Miss B. has never been married. She is nearly six feet high; she loves waltzing beyond even poesy; and I think lobster-salad as much as either. She confesses to twenty-eight; in which case her first volume, "The Orphan of Gozo," (cut up by Mr. Rigby, in the Quarterly, with his usual kindness,) must have been published when she was three years old.

For a woman all soul, she certainly eats as much as any woman I ever saw. The sufferings she has had to endure, are, she says, beyond compare; the poems which she writes breathe a withering passion, a smouldering despair, an agony of spirit that would melt the soul of a drayman, were he to read them. Well, it is a comfort to see that she can dance of nights, and to know (for the habits of illustrious literary persons are always worth knowing) that she eats a hot mutton-chop for breakfast every morning of her blighted existence.

She lives in a boardinghouse at Brompton, and comes to the party in a fly.

MR. HICKS.

It is worth twopence to see Miss Bunion and Poseidon Hicks, the great poet, conversing with one another, and to talk of one to the other afterwards. How they hate each other! I (in my wicked way) have sent Hicks almost raving mad, by praising Bunion to him in confidence; and you can drive Bunion out of the room by a few judicious panegyrics of Hicks.

Hicks first burst upon the astonished world with poems, in the Byronic manner: "The Death-Shriek," "The Bastard of Lara," "The Atabal," "The Fire-Ship of Botzaris," and other works. His "Love Lays," in Mr. Moore's early style, were pronounced to be wonderfully precocious for a young gentleman then only thirteen, and in a commercial academy, at Tooting.

Subsequently, this great bard became less passionate and more thoughtful; and, at the age of twenty, wrote "Idiosyncracy" (in forty books, 4to.):

"Ararat," "a stupendous epic," as the reviews said; and "The Megatheria," "a magnificent contribution to our pre-Adamite literature," according to the same authorities. Not having read these works, it would ill become me to judge them; but I know that poor Jingle, the publisher, always attributed his insolvency to the latter epic, which was magnificently printed in elephant folio.

Hicks has now taken a classical turn, and has brought out "Poseidon," "Iacchus," "Hephaestus," and I dare say is going through the mythology. But I should not like to try him at a passage of the Greek Delectus, any more than twenty thousand others of us who have had a "classical education."

Hicks was taken in an inspired attitude regarding the chandelier, and pretending he didn't know that Miss Pettifer was looking at him.

Her name is Anna Maria (daughter of Higgs and Pettifer, solicitors, Bedford Row); but Hicks calls her "Ianthe" in his album verses, and is himself an eminent drysalter in the city.

MISS MEGGOT.

Poor Miss Meggot is not so lucky as Miss Bunion. Nobody comes to dance with HER, though she has a new frock on, as she calls it, and rather a pretty foot, which she always manages to stick out.

She is forty-seven, the youngest of three sisters, who live a mouldy old house, near Middlesex Hospital, where they have lived for I don't know how many score of years; but this is certain: the eldest Miss Meggot saw the Gordon Riots out of that same parlor window, and tells the story how her father (physician to George III.) was robbed of his queue in the streets on that occasion. The two old ladies have taken the brevet rank, and are addressed as Mrs. Jane and Mrs. Betsy: one of them is at whist in the back drawing-room. But the youngest is still called Miss Nancy, and is considered quite a baby by her sisters.

She was going to be married once to a brave young officer, Ensign Angus Macquirk, of the Whistlebinkie Fencibles; but he fell at Quatre Bras, by the side of the gallant Snuffmull, his commander. Deeply, deeply did Miss Nancy deplore him.

But time has cicatrized the wounded heart. She is gay now, and would sing or dance, ay, or marry if anybody asked her.

Do go, my dear friend--I don't mean to ask her to marry, but to ask her to dance.--Never mind the looks of the thing. It will make her happy; and what does it cost you? Ah, my dear fellow! take this counsel: always dance with the old ladies--always dance with the governesses. It is a comfort to the poor things when they get up in their garret that somebody has had mercy on them. And such a handsome fellow as YOU too!

MISS RANVILLE, REV. MR. TOOP, MISS MULLINS, MR. WINTER.

Mr. W. Miss Mullins, look at Miss Ranville: what a picture of good humor.

Miss M. Oh, you satirical creature!

Mr. W. Do you know why she is so angry? she expected to dance with Captain Grig, and by some mistake, the Cambridge Professor got hold of her: isn't he a handsome man?

Miss M. Oh, you droll wretch!

Mr. W. Yes, he's a fellow of college, fellows mayn't marry, Miss Mullins, poor fellows, ay, Miss Mullins?

Miss M. -La!

Mr. W. And Professor of Phlebotomy in the University. He flatters himself he is a man of the world, Miss Mullins, and always dances in the long vacation.

Miss M. You malicious, wicked monster!

Mr. W. Do you know Lady Jane Ranville? Miss Ranville's mamma. A ball once a year; footmen in canary-colored livery: Baker Street; six dinners in the season; starves all the year round; pride and poverty, you know; I've been to her ball ONCE. Ranville Ranville's her brother, and between you and me but this, dear Miss Mullins, is a profound secret, I think he's a greater fool than his sister.

Miss M. Oh, you satirical, droll, malicious, wicked thing you!

Mr. W. You do me injustice, Miss Mullins, indeed you do.

[Chaine Anglaise.]

MISS JOY, MR. AND MRS. JOY, MR. BOTTER.

Mr. B. What spirits that girl has, Mrs. Joy!

Mr. J. She's a sunshine in a house, Botter, a regular sunshine. When Mrs. J. here's in a bad humor, I . . .

Mrs. J. Don't talk nonsense, Mr. Joy.

Mrs. B. There's a hop, skip, and jump for you! Why, it beats Ellsler! Upon my conscience it does! It's her fourteenth quadrille too. There she goes! She's a jewel of a girl, though I say it that shouldn't.

Mrs. J. (laughing). Why don't you marry her, Botter? Shall I speak to her? I dare say she'd have you. You're not so VERY old.

Mr. B. Don't aggravate me, Mrs. J. You know when I lost my heart in the year 1817, at the opening of Waterloo Bridge, to a young lady who wouldn't have me, and left me to die in despair, and married Joy, of the Stock Exchange.

Mrs. J. Get away, you foolish old creature.

[MR. JOY looks on in ecstasies at Miss Joy's agility. LADY JANE RANVILLE, of Baker Street, pronounces her to be an exceedingly forward person. CAPTAIN DOBBS likes a girl who has plenty of go in her; and as for FRED SPARKS, he is over head and ears in love with her.]

MR. RANVILLE RANVILLE AND JACK HUBBARD.

This is Miss Ranville Ranville's brother, Mr. Ranville Ranville, of the Foreign Office, faithfully designed as he was playing at whist in the card-room. Talleyrand used to play at whist at the "Travellers'," that is why Ranville Ranville indulges in that diplomatic recreation. It is not his fault if he be not the greatest man in the room.

If you speak to him, he smiles sternly, and answers in monosyllables he would rather die than commit himself. He never has committed himself in his life. He was the first at school, and distinguished at Oxford. He is growing prematurely bald now, like Canning, and is quite proud of it. He rides in St. James's Park of a morning before breakfast. He dockets his tailor's bills, and nicks off his dinner-notes in diplomatic paragraphs, and keeps precis of them all. If he ever makes a joke, it is a quotation from Horace, like Sir Robert Peel. The only relaxation he permits himself, is to read Thucydides in the holidays.

Everybody asks him out to dinner, on account of his brass-buttons with the Queen's cipher, and to have the air of being well with the Foreign Office. "Where I dine," he says solemnly, "I think it is my duty to go to evening-parties." That is why he is here. He never dances, never sups, never drinks. He has gruel when he goes home to bed. I think it is in his brains.

He is such an ass and so respectable, that one wonders he has not succeeded in the world; and yet somehow they laugh at him; and you and I shall be Ministers as soon as he will.

Yonder, making believe to look over the print-books, is that merry rogue, Jack Hubbard.

See how jovial he looks! He is the life and soul of every party, and his impromptu singing after supper will make you die of laughing. He is meditating an impromptu now, and at the same time thinking about a bill that is coming due next Thursday. Happy dog!

MRS. TROTTER, MISS TROTTER, MISS TOADY, LORD METHUSELAH.

Dear Emma Trotter has been silent and rather ill-humored all the evening until now her pretty face lights up with smiles. Cannot you guess why? Pity the simple and affectionate creature! Lord Methuselah has not arrived until this moment: and see how the artless girl steps forward to greet him!

In the midst of all the selfishness and turmoil of the world, how charming it is to find virgin hearts quite unsullied, and to look on at little romantic pictures of mutual love! Lord Methuselah, though you know his age by the peerage--though he is old, wigged, gouty, rouged, wicked, has lighted up a pure flame in that gentle bosom. There was a talk about Tom Willoughby last year; and then, for a time, young Hawbuck (Sir John Hawbuck's youngest son) seemed the favored man; but Emma never knew her mind until she met the dear creature before you in a Rhine steamboat. "Why are you so late, Edward?" says she. Dear artless child!

Her mother looks on with tender satisfaction. One can appreciate the joys of such an admirable parent!

"Look at them!" says Miss Toady. "I vow and protest they're the handsomest couple in the room!"

Methuselah's grandchildren are rather jealous and angry, and Mademoiselle Ariane, of the French theatre, is furious. But there's no accounting for the mercenary envy of some people; and it is impossible to satisfy everybody.

MR. BEAUMORIS, MR. GRIG, MR. FLYNDERS.

Those three young men are described in a twinkling: Captain Grig of the Heavies; Mr. Beaumoris, the handsome young man; Tom Flinders (Flynders Flynders he now calls himself), the fat gentleman who dresses after Beaumoris.

Beaumoris is in the Treasury: he has a salary of eighty pounds a year, on which he maintains the best cab and horses of the season; and out of which he pays seventy guineas merely for his subscriptions to clubs. He hunts in Leicestershire, where great men mount him; he is a prodigious favorite behind the scenes at the theatres; you may get glimpses of him at Richmond, with all sorts of pink bonnets; and he is the sworn friend of half the most famous roues about town, such as Old Methuselah, Lord Billygoat, Lord Tarquin, and the rest: a respectable race. It is to oblige the former that the good-natured young fellow is here to-night; though it must not be imagined that he gives himself any airs of superiority. Dandy as he is, he is quite affable, and would borrow ten guineas from any man in the room, in the most jovial way possible.

It is neither Beau's birth, which is doubtful; nor his money, which is entirely negative; nor his honesty, which goes along with his money-qualification; nor his wit, for he can barely spell, which recommend him to the fashionable world: but a sort of Grand Seigneur splendor and dandified je ne scais quoi, which make the man he is of him. The way in which his boots and gloves fit him is a wonder which no other man can achieve; and though he has not an atom of principle, it must be confessed that he invented the Taglioni shirt.

When I see these magnificent dandies yawning out of "White's," or caracoling in the Park on shining chargers, I like to think that Brummell was the greatest of them all, and that Brummell's father was a footman.

Flynders is Beaumoris's toady: lends him money: buys horses through his recommendation; dresses after him; clings to him in Pall Mall, and on the steps of the club; and talks about 'Bo' in all societies. It is his drag which carries down Bo's friends to the Derby, and his cheques pay for dinners to the pink bonnets. I don't believe the Perkinses know what a rogue it is, but fancy him a decent, reputable City man, like his father before him.

As for Captain Grig, what is there to tell about him? He performs the duties of his calling with perfect gravity. He is faultless on parade; excellent across country; amiable when drunk, rather slow when sober. He has not two ideas, and is a most good-natured, irreproachable, gallant, and stupid young officer.

CAVALIER SEUL.

This is my friend Bob Hely, performing the Cavalier seul in a quadrille. Remark the good-humored pleasure depicted in his countenance. Has he any secret grief? Has he a pain anywhere? No, dear Miss Jones, he is dancing like a true Briton, and with all the charming gayety and abandon of our race.

When Canaillard performs that Cavalier seul operation, does HE flinch? No: he puts on his most vainqueur look, he sticks his thumbs into the armholes of his waistcoat, and advances, retreats, pirouettes, and otherwise gambadoes, as though to say, "Regarde moi, O monde! Venez, O femmes, venez voir danser Canaillard!"

When De Bobwitz executes the same measure, he does it with smiling agility, and graceful ease.

But poor Hely, if he were advancing to a dentist, his face would not be more cheerful. All the eyes of the room are upon him, he thinks; and he thinks he looks like a fool.

Upon my word, if you press the point with me, dear Miss Jones, I think he is not very far from right. I think that while Frenchmen and Germans may dance, as it is their nature to do, there is a natural dignity about us Britons, which debars us from that enjoyment. I am rather of the Turkish opinion, that this should be done for us. I think . . .

"Good-by, you envious old fox-and-the-grapes," says Miss Jones, and the next moment I see her whirling by in a polka with Tom Tozer, at a pace which makes me shrink back with terror into the little boudoir.

M. CANAILLARD, CHEVALIER OF THE LEGION OF HONOR.

LIEUTENANT BARON DE BOBWITZ.

Canaillard. Oh, ces Anglais! quels hommes, mon Dieu! Comme ils sont habilles, comme ils dansent!

Bobwitz. Ce sont de beaux hommes bourtant; point de tenue militaire, mais de grands gaillards; si je les avais dans ma compagnie de la Garde, j'en ferai de bons soldats.

Canaillard. Est-il bete, cet Allemand! Les grands hommes ne font pas toujours de bons soldats, Monsieur. Il me semble que les soldats de France qui sont de ma taille, Monsieur, valent un peu mieux . . .

Bobwitz. Vous croyez?

Canaillard. Comment! je le crois, Monsieur? J'en suis sur! Il me semble, Monsieur, que nous l'avons prouve.

Bobwitz (impatiently). Je m'en vais danser la Bolka. Serviteur, Monsieur.

Canaillard. Butor! (He goes and looks at himself in the glass, when he is seized by Mrs. Perkins for the Polka.)

THE BOUDOIR.

MR. SMITH, MR. BROWN, MISS BUSTLETON.

Mr. Brown. You polk, Miss Bustleton? I'm SO delaighted.

Miss Bustleton. [Smiles and prepares to rise.]

Mr. Smith. D - puppy.

(Poor Smith don't polk.)

GRAND POLKA.

Though a quadrille seems to me as dreary as a funeral, yet to look at a polka, I own, is pleasant. See! Brown and Emily Bustleton are whirling round as light as two pigeons over a dovecot; Tozer, with that wicked whisking little Jones, spins along as merrily as a May-day sweep; Miss Joy is the partner of the happy Fred Sparks; and even Miss Ranville is pleased, for the faultless Captain Grig is toe and heel with her. Beaumoris, with rather a nonchalant air, takes a turn with Miss Trotter, at which Lord Methuseleh's wrinkled chops quiver uneasily. See! how the big Baron de Bobwitz spins lightly, and gravely, and gracefully round; and lo! the Frenchman staggering under the weight of Miss Bunion, who tramps and kicks like a young cart-horse.

But the most awful sight which met my view in this dance was the unfortunate Miss Little, to whom fate had assigned THE MULLIGAN as a partner. Like a pavid kid in the talons of an eagle, that young creature trembled in his huge Milesian grasp. Disdaining the recognized form of the dance, the Irish chieftain accommodated the music to the dance of his own green land, and performed a double shuffle jig, carrying Miss Little along with him. Miss Ranville and her Captain shrank back amazed; Miss Trotter skirried out of his way into the protection of the astonished Lord Methuselah; Fred Sparks could hardly move for laughing; while, on the contrary, Miss Joy was quite in pain for poor Sophy Little. As Canaillard and the Poetess came up, The Mulligan, in the height of his enthusiasm, lunged out a kick which sent Miss Bunion howling; and concluded with a tremendous Hurroo! a war-cry which caused every Saxon heart to shudder and quail.

"Oh that the earth would open and kindly take me in!" I exclaimed mentally; and slunk off into the lower regions, where by this time half the company were at supper.

THE SUPPER.

The supper is going on behind the screen. There is no need to draw the supper. We all know that sort of transaction: the squabbling, and gobbling, and popping of champagne; the smell of musk and lobster-salad; the dowagers chumping away at plates of raised pie; the young lassies nibbling at little titbits, which the dexterous young gentlemen procure. Three large men, like doctors of divinity, wait behind the table, and furnish everything that appetite can ask for. I never, for my part, can eat any supper for wondering at those men. I believe if you were to ask them for mashed turnips, or a slice of crocodile, those astonishing people would serve you. What a contempt they must have for the guttling crowd to whom they minister, those solemn pastry-cook's men! How they must hate jellies, and game-pies, and champagne, in their hearts! How they must scorn my poor friend Grundsell behind the screen, who is sucking at a bottle!

This disguised green-grocer is a very well-known character in the neighborhood of Pocklington Square. He waits at the parties of the gentry in the neighborhood, and though, of course, despised in families where a footman is kept, is a person of much importance in female establishments.

Miss Jonas always employs him at her parties, and says to her page, "Vincent, send the butler, or send Desborough to me;" by which name she chooses to designate G. G.

When the Miss Frumps have post-horses to their carriage, and pay visits, Grundsell always goes behind. Those ladies have the greatest confidence in him, have been godmothers to fourteen of his children, and leave their house in his charge when they go to Bognor for the summer. He attended those ladies when they were presented at the last drawing-room of her Majesty Queen Charlotte.

GEORGE GRUNDSELL,

GREEN-GROCER AND SALESMAN,

9, LITTLE POCKLINGTON BUILDINGS,

LATE CONFIDENTIAL SERVANT IN THE FAMILY OF

THE LORD MAYOR OF LONDON.

Carpets Beat. Knives and Boots cleaned per contract. Errands faithfully performed, G. G. attends Ball and Dinner parties, and from his knowledge of the most distinguished Families in London, confidently recommends his services to the distinguished neighbourhood of Pocklington Square.

Mr. Grundsell's state costume is a blue coat and copper buttons, a white waistcoat, and an immense frill and shirt-collar. He was for many years a private watchman, and once canvassed for the office of parish clerk of St. Peter's Pocklington. He can be intrusted with untold spoons; with anything, in fact, but liquor; and it was he who brought round the cards for MRS. PERKINS'S BALL.

AFTER SUPPER.

I do not intend to say any more about it. After the people had supped, they went back and danced. Some supped again. I gave Miss Bunion, with my own hands, four bumpers of champagne: and such a quantity of goose-liver and truffles, that I don't wonder she took a glass of cherry-brandy afterwards. The gray morning was in Pocklington Square as she drove away in her fly. So did the other people go away. How green and sallow some of the girls looked, and how awfully clear Mrs. Colonel Bludyer's rouge was! Lady Jane Ranville's great coach had roared away down the streets long before. Fred Minchin pattered off in his clogs: it was I who covered up Miss Meggot, and conducted her, with her two old sisters, to the carriage. Good old souls! They have shown their gratitude by asking me to tea next Tuesday. Methuselah is gone to finish the night at the club. "Mind to-morrow," Miss Trotter says, kissing her hand out of the carriage. Canaillard departs, asking the way to "Lesterre Squar." They all go away, life goes away.

Look at Miss Martin and young Ward! How tenderly the rogue is wrapping her up! how kindly she looks at him! The old folks are whispering behind as they wait for their carriage. What is their talk, think you? and when shall that pair make a match? When you see those pretty little creatures with their smiles and their blushes, and their pretty ways, would you like to be the Grand Bashaw?

"Mind and send me a large piece of cake," I go up and whisper archly to old Mr. Ward: and we look on rather sentimentally at the couple, almost the last in the rooms (there, I declare, go the musicians, and the clock is at five) when Grundsell, with an air effare, rushes up to me and says, "For e'v'n sake, sir, go into the supper-room: there's that Hirish gent a-pitchin' into Mr. P."

THE MULLIGAN AND MR. PERKINS.

It was too true. I had taken him away after supper (he ran after Miss Little's carriage, who was dying in love with him as he fancied), but the brute had come back again. The doctors of divinity were putting up their condiments: everybody was gone; but the abominable Mulligan sat swinging his legs at the lonely supper-table!

Perkins was opposite, gasping at him.

The Mulligan. I tell ye, ye are the butler, ye big fat man. Go get me some more champagne: it's good at this house.

Mr. Perkins (with dignity). It IS good at this house; but-

The Mulligan. Bht hwhat, ye goggling, bow-windowed jackass? Go get the wine, and we'll dthrink it together, my old buck.

Mr. Perkins. My name, sir, is PERKINS.

The Mulligan. Well, that rhymes with jerkins, my man of firkins; so don't let us have any more shirkings and lurkings, Mr. Perkins.

Mr. Perkins (with apoplectic energy). Sir, I am the master of this house; and I order you to quit it. I'll not be insulted, sir. I'll send for a policeman, sir. What do you mean, Mr. Titmarsh, sir, by bringing this, this beast into my house, sir?

At this, with a scream like that of a Hyrcanian tiger, Mulligan of the hundred battles sprang forward at his prey; but we were beforehand with him. Mr. Gregory, Mr. Grundsell, Sir Giles Bacon's large man, the young gentlemen, and myself, rushed simultaneously upon the tipsy chieftain, and confined him. The doctors of divinity looked on with perfect indifference. That Mr. Perkins did not go off in a fit is a wonder. He was led away heaving and snorting frightfully.

Somebody smashed Mulligan's hat over his eyes, and I led him forth into the silent morning. The chirrup of the birds, the freshness of the rosy air, and a penn'orth of coffee that I got for him at a stall in the Regent Circus, revived him somewhat. When I quitted him, he was not angry but sad. He was desirous, it is true, of avenging the wrongs of Erin in battle line; he wished also to share the grave of Sarsfield and Hugh O'Neill; but he was sure that Miss Perkins, as well as Miss Little, was desperately in love with him; and I left him on a doorstep in tears.

"Is it best to be laughing-mad, or crying-mad, in the world?" says I moodily, coming into my street. Betsy the maid was already up and at work, on her knees, scouring the steps, and cheerfully beginning her honest daily labor.

The Notch On The Ax

I

Everyone remembers in the Fourth Book of the immortal poem of your Blind Bard (to whose sightless orbs no doubt Glorious Shapes were apparent, and Visions Celestial), how Adam discourses to Eve of the Bright Visitors who hovered round their Eden-

'Millions of spiritual creatures walk the earth,
Unseen, both when we wake and when we sleep.'

"'How often,' says Father Adam, 'from the steep of echoing hill or thicket, have we heard celestial voices to the midnight air, sole, or responsive to each other's notes, singing!' After the Act of Disobedience, when the erring pair from Eden took their solitary way, and went forth to toil and trouble on common earth, though the Glorious Ones no longer were visible, you cannot say they were gone. It was not that the Bright Ones were absent, but that the dim eyes of rebel man no longer could see them. In your chamber hangs a picture of one whom you never knew, but whom you have long held in tenderest regard, and who was painted for you by a friend of mine, the Knight of Plympton. She communes with you. She smiles on you. When your spirits are low, her bright eyes shine on you and cheer you. Her innocent sweet smile is a caress to you. She never fails to soothe you with her speechless prattle. You love her. She is alive with you. As you extinguish your candle and turn to sleep, though your eyes see her not, is she not there still smiling? As you lie in the night awake, and thinking of your duties, and the morrow's inevitable toil oppressing the busy, weary, wakeful brain as with a remorse, the crackling fire flashes up for a moment in the grate, and she is there, your little Beauteous Maiden, smiling with her sweet eyes! When moon is down, when fire is out, when curtains are drawn, when lids are closed, is she not there, the little Beautiful One, though invisible, present and smiling still? Friend, the Unseen Ones are round about us. Does it not seem as if the time were drawing near when it shall be given to men to behold them?"

The print of which my friend spoke, and which, indeed, hangs in my room, though he has never been there, is that charming little winter piece of Sir Joshua, representing the little Lady Caroline Montague, afterwards Duchess of Buccleuch. She is represented as standing in the midst of a winter landscape, wrapped in muff and cloak; and she looks out of her picture with a smile so exquisite that a Herod could not see her without being charmed.

"I beg your pardon, Mr. PINTO," I said to the person with whom I was conversing. (I wonder, by the way, that I was not surprised at his knowing how fond I am of this print.) "You spoke of the Knight of Plympton. Sir Joshua died 1792: and you say he was your dear friend?"

As I spoke I chanced to look at Mr. Pinto; and then it suddenly struck me: Gracious powers! Perhaps you ARE a hundred years old, now I think of it. You look more than a hundred. Yes, you may be a thousand years old for what I know. Your teeth are false. One eye is evidently false. Can I say that the other is not? If a man's age may be calculated by the rings round his eyes, this man may be as old as Methuselah. He has no beard. He wears a large curly glossy brown wig, and his eyebrows are painted a deep olive-green. It was odd to hear this man, this walking mummy, talking sentiment, in these queer old chambers in Shepherd's Inn.

Pinto passed a yellow bandanna handkerchief over his awful white teeth, and kept his glass eye steadily fixed on me. "Sir Joshua's friend?" said he (you perceive, eluding my direct question). "Is not everyone that knows his pictures Reynolds's friend? Suppose I tell you that I have been in his painting room scores of times, and that his sister The has made me tea, and his sister Toffy has made coffee for me? You will only say I am an old ombog." (Mr. Pinto, I remarked, spoke all languages with an accent equally foreign.)

"Suppose I tell you that I knew Mr. Sam Johnson, and did not like him? that I was at that very ball at Madame Cornelis', which you have mentioned in one of your little, what do you call them? bah! my memory begins to fail me, in one of your little Whirligig Papers? Suppose I tell you that Sir Joshua has been here, in this very room?"

"Have you, then, had these apartments for more than seventy years?" I asked.

"They look as if they had not been swept for that time, don't they? Hey? I did not say that I had them for seventy years, but that Sir Joshua has visited me here."

"When?" I asked, eying the man sternly, for I began to think he was an impostor.

He answered me with a glance still more stern: "Sir Joshua Reynolds was here this very morning, with Angelica Kaufmann and Mr. Oliver Goldschmidt. He is still very much attached to Angelica, who still does not care for him. Because he is dead (and I was in the fourth mourning coach at his funeral) is that any reason why he should not come back to earth again? My good sir, you are laughing at me. He has sat many a time on that very chair which you are now occupying. There are several spirits in the room now, whom you cannot see. Excuse me." Here he turned round as if he was addressing somebody, and began rapidly speaking a language unknown to me. "It is Arabic," he said; "a bad patois, I own. I learned it in Barbary, when I was a prisoner among the Moors. In anno 1609, bin ick Aldus ghekledt gheghaen. Ha! you doubt me: look at me well. At least I am like-"

Perhaps some of my readers remember a paper of which the figure of a man carrying a barrel formed the initial letter, and which I copied from an old spoon now in my possession. As I looked at Mr. Pinto I do declare he looked so like the figure on that old piece of plate that I started and felt very uneasy. "Ha!" said he, laughing through his false teeth (I declare they were false – I could see utterly toothless gums working up and down behind the pink coral), "you see I wore a beard den; I am shafed now; perhaps you tink I am A SPOON. Ha, ha!" And as he laughed he gave a cough which I thought would have coughed his teeth out, his glass eye out, his wig off, his very head off; but he stopped this convulsion by stumping across the room and seizing a little bottle of bright pink medicine, which, being opened, spread a singular acrid aromatic odor through the apartment; and I thought I saw but of this I cannot take an affirmation, a light green and violet flame flickering round the neck of the vial as he opened it. By the way, from the peculiar stumping noise which he made in crossing the bare-boarded apartment, I knew at once that my strange entertainer had a wooden leg. Over the dust which lay quite thick on the boards, you could see the mark of one foot very neat and pretty, and then a round O, which was naturally the impression made by the wooden stump. I own I had a queer thrill as I saw that mark, and felt a secret comfort that it was not CLOVEN.

In this desolate apartment in which Mr. Pinto had invited me to see him, there were three chairs, one bottomless, a little table on which you might put a breakfast tray, and not a single other article of furniture. In the next room, the door of which was open, I could see a magnificent gilt dressing case, with some splendid diamond and ruby shirt studs lying by it, and a chest of drawers, and a cupboard apparently full of clothes.

Remembering him in Baden-Baden in great magnificence I wondered at his present denuded state. "You have a house elsewhere, Mr. Pinto?" I said.

"Many," says he. "I have apartments in many cities. I lock dem up, and do not carry mosh logish."

I then remembered that his apartment at Baden, where I first met him, was bare, and had no bed in it.

"There is, then, a sleeping room beyond?"

"This is the sleeping room." (He pronounces it DIS. Can this, by the way, give any clew to the nationality of this singular man?)

"If you sleep on these two old chairs you have a rickety couch; if on the floor, a dusty one."

"Suppose I sleep up dere?" said this strange man, and he actually pointed up to the ceiling. I thought him mad or what he himself called "an ombog." "I know. You do not believe me; for why should I deceive you? I came but to propose a matter of business to you. I told you I could give you the clew to the mystery of the Two Children in Black, whom you met at Baden, and you came to see me. If I told you you would not believe me. What for try and convinz you? Ha hey?" And he shook his hand once, twice, thrice, at me, and glared at me out of his eye in a peculiar way.

Of what happened now I protest I cannot give an accurate account. It seemed to me that there shot a flame from his eye into my brain, while behind his GLASS eye there was a green illumination as if a candle had been lit in it. It seemed to me that from his long fingers two quivering flames issued, sputtering, as it were, which penetrated me, and forced me back into one of the chairs, the broken one, out of which I had much difficulty in scrambling, when the strange glamour was ended. It seemed to me that, when I was so fixed, so transfixed in the broken chair, the man floated up to the ceiling, crossed his legs, folded his arms as if he was lying on a sofa, and grinned down at me. When I came to myself he was down from the ceiling, and, taking me out of the broken cane-bottomed chair, kindly enough "Bah!" said he, "it is the smell of my medicine. It often gives the vertigo. I thought you would have had a little fit. Come into the open air." And we went down the steps, and into Shepherd's Inn, where the setting sun was just shining on the statue of Shepherd; the laundresses were traipsing about; the porters were leaning against the railings; and the clerks were playing at marbles, to my inexpressible consolation.

"You said you were going to dine at the 'Gray's-Inn Coffee-House,'" he said. I was. I often dine there. There is excellent wine at the "Gray's-Inn Coffee-House"; but I declare I NEVER SAID so. I was not astonished at his remark; no more astonished than if I was in a dream. Perhaps I WAS in a dream. Is life a dream? Are dreams facts? Is sleeping being really awake? I don't know. I tell you I am puzzled. I have read "The Woman in White," "The Strange Story" not to mention that story "Stranger than Fiction" in the Cornhill Magazine, that story for which THREE credible witnesses are ready to vouch. I have had messages from the dead; and not only from the dead, but from people who never existed at all. I own I am in a state of much bewilderment: but, if you please, will proceed with my simple, my artless story.

Well, then. We passed from Shepherd's Inn into Holborn, and looked for a while at Woodgate's bric-a-brac shop, which I never can pass without delaying at the windows, indeed, if I were going to be hung, I would beg the cart to stop, and let me have one look more at that delightful omnium gatherum. And passing Woodgate's, we come to Gale's little shop, "No. 47," which is also a favourite haunt of mine.

Mr. Gale happened to be at his door, and as we exchanged salutations, "Mr. Pinto," I said, "will you like to see a real curiosity in this curiosity shop? Step into Mr. Gale's little back room."

In that little back parlor there are Chinese gongs; there are old Saxe and Sevres plates; there is Furstenberg, Carl Theodor, Worcester, Amstel, Nankin and other jimcrockery. And in the corner what do you think there is? There is an actual GUILLOTINE. If you doubt me, go and see - Gale, High Holborn, No. 47. It is a slim instrument, much slighter than those which they make now; some nine feet high, narrow, a pretty piece of upholstery enough. There is the hook over which the rope used to play which unloosened the dreadful ax above; and look! dropped into the orifice where the head used to go - there is THE AX itself, all rusty, with A GREAT NOTCH IN THE BLADE.

As Pinto looked at it, Mr. Gale was not in the room, I recollect; happening to have been just called out by a customer who offered him three pound fourteen and sixpence for a blue Shepherd in pate tendre, Mr. Pinto gave a little start, and seemed crispe for a moment. Then he looked steadily toward one of those great porcelain stools which you see in gardens and it seemed to me I tell you I won't take my affidavit, I may have been maddened by the six glasses I took of that pink elixir, I may have been sleep-walking: perhaps am as I write now, I may have been under the influence of that astounding MEDIUM into whose hands I had fallen but I vow I heard Pinto say, with rather a ghastly grin at the porcelain stool,

"Nay, nefer shague your gory locks at me, Dou canst not say I did it."

(He pronounced it, by the way, I DIT it, by which I KNOW that Pinto was a German.)

I heard Pinto say those very words, and sitting on the porcelain stool I saw, dimly at first, then with an awful distinctness – a ghost - an EIDOLON - a form - A HEADLESS MAN seated with his head in his lap, which wore an expression of piteous surprise.

At this minute, Mr. Gale entered from the front shop to show a customer some Delft plates; and he did not see but WE DID – the figure rise up from the porcelain stool, shake its head, which it held in its hand, and which kept its eyes fixed sadly on us, and disappear behind the guillotine.

"Come to the 'Gray's-Inn Coffee-House,'" Pinto said, "and I will tell you how the notch came to the ax." And we walked down Holborn at about thirty-seven minutes past six o'clock.

If there is anything in the above statement which astonishes the reader, I promise him that in the next chapter of this little story he will be astonished still more.

II

"You will excuse me," I said to my companion, "for remarking that when you addressed the individual sitting on the porcelain stool, with his head in his lap, your ordinarily benevolent features" (this I confess was a bouncer, for between ourselves a more sinister and ill-looking rascal than Mons. P. I have seldom set eyes on) "your ordinarily handsome face wore an expression that was by no means pleasing. You grinned at the individual just as you did at me when you went up to the cei-, pardon me, as I THOUGHT you did, when I fell down in a fit in your chambers"; and I qualified my words in a great flutter and tremble; I did not care to offend the man, I did not DARE to offend the man. I thought once or twice of jumping into a cab, and flying; of taking refuge in Day and Martin's Blacking Warehouse; of speaking to a policeman, but not one would come. I was this man's slave. I followed him like his dog. I COULD not get away from him. So, you see, I went on meanly conversing with him, and affecting a simpering confidence. I remember, when I was a little boy at school, going up fawning and smiling in this way to some great hulking bully of a sixth-form boy. So I said in a word, "Your ordinarily handsome face wore a disagreeable expression," &c.

"It is ordinarily VERY handsome," said he, with such a leer at a couple of passers-by, that one of them cried, "Oh, crickey, here's a precious guy!" and a child, in its nurse's arms, screamed itself into convulsions. "Oh, oui, che suis tres-choli garcon, bien peau, cerdainement," continued Mr. Pinto; "but you were right. That, that person was not very well pleased when he saw me. There was no love lost between us, as you say: and the world never knew a more worthless miscreant. I hate him, voyez-vous? I hated him alife; I hate him dead. I hate him man; I hate him ghost: and he know it, and tremble before me. If I see him twenty tausend years hence and why not? I shall hate him still. You remarked how he was dressed?"

"In black satin breeches and striped stockings; a white pique waistcoat, a gray coat, with large metal buttons, and his hair in powder. He must have worn a pigtail - only-"

"Only it was CUT OFF! Ha, ha, ha!" Mr. Pinto cried, yelling a laugh, which I observed made the policeman stare very much. "Yes. It was cut off by the same blow which took off the scoundrel's Head - ho, ho, ho!" And he made a circle with his hook-nailed finger round his own yellow neck, and grinned with a horrible triumph. "I promise you that fellow was surprised when he found his head in the pannier. Ha! ha! Do you ever cease to hate those whom you hate?" fire flashed terrifically from his glass eye as he spoke "or to love dose whom you once loved? Oh, never, never!" And here his natural eye was bedewed with tears. "But here we are at the 'Gray's-Inn CoffeeHouse.' James, what is the joint?"

That very respectful and efficient waiter brought in the bill of fare, and I, for my part, chose boiled leg of pork, and pease pudding, which my acquaintance said would do as well as anything else; though I remarked he only trifled with the pease pudding, and left all the pork on the plate. In fact, he scarcely ate anything. But he drank a prodigious quantity of wine; and I must say that my friend Mr. Hart's port wine is so good that I myself took, well, I should think, I took three glasses. Yes, three, certainly. HE – I mean Mr. P. the old rogue, was insatiable: for we had to call for a second bottle in no time. When that was gone, my companion wanted another. A little red mounted up to his yellow cheeks as he drank the wine, and he winked at it in a strange manner. "I remember," said he, musing, "when port wine was scarcely drunk in this country though the Queen liked it, and so did Hurley; but Bolingbroke didn't, he drank Florence and Champagne. Dr. Swift put water to his wine. 'Jonathan,' I once said to him but bah! Autres temps, autres moeurs. Another magnum, James."

This was all very well. "My good sir," I said, "it may suit YOU to order bottles of '20 port, at a guinea a bottle; but that kind of price does not suit me. I only happen to have thirty-four and sixpence in my pocket, of which I want a shilling for the waiter, and eighteen pence for my cab. You rich foreigners and SWELLS may spend what you like" (I had him there: for my friend's dress was as shabby as an old-clothes man's); "but a man with a family, Mr. Whatd'you-call'im, cannot afford to spend seven or eight hundred a year on his dinner alone."

"Bah!" he said. "Nunkey pays for all, as you say. I will what you call stant the dinner, if you are SO POOR!" and again he gave that disagreeable grin, and placed an odious crook-nailed and by no means clean finger to his nose. But I was not so afraid of him now, for we were in a public place; and the three glasses of port wine had, you see, given me courage.

"What a pretty snuff-box!" he remarked, as I handed him mine, which I am still old-fashioned enough to carry. It is a pretty old gold box enough, but valuable to me especially as a relic of an old, old relative, whom I can just remember as a child, when she was very kind to me. "Yes; a pretty box. I can remember when many ladies, most ladies, carried a box, nay, two boxes, tabatiere and bonbonniere. What lady carries snuff-box now, hey? Suppose your astonishment if a lady in an assembly were to offer you a prise? I can remember a lady with such a box as this, with a tour, as we used to call it then; with paniers, with a tortoise-shell cane, with the prettiest little high-heeled velvet shoes in the world! ah! that was a time, that was a time! Ah, Eliza, Eliza, I have thee now in my mind's eye! At Bungay on the Waveney, did I not walk with thee, Eliza? Aha, did I not love thee? Did I not walk with thee then? Do I not see thee still?"

This was passing strange. My ancestress but there is no need to publish her revered name, did indeed live at Bungay St. Mary's, where she lies buried. She used to walk with a tortoise-shell cane. She used to wear little black velvet shoes, with the prettiest high heels in the world.

"Did you-did you-know, then, my great-gr-nd-m-ther?" I said.

He pulled up his coat sleeve "Is that her name?" he said.

"Eliza-"

There, I declare, was the very name of the kind old creature written in red on his arm.

"YOU knew her old," he said, divining my thoughts (with his strange knack); "I knew her young and lovely. I danced with her at the Bury ball. Did I not, dear, dear Miss ----?"

As I live, he here mentioned dear gr-nny's MAIDEN name. Her maiden name was ----. Her honored married name was ----.

"She married your great-gr-ndf-th-r the year Poseidon won the Newmarket Plate," Mr. Pinto dryly remarked.

Merciful powers! I remember, over the old shagreen knife and spoon case on the sideboard in my gr-nny's parlor, a print by Stubbs of that very horse. My grandsire, in a red coat, and his fair hair flowing over his shoulders, was over the mantelpiece, and Poseidon won the Newmarket Cup in the year 1783!

"Yes; you are right. I danced a minuet with her at Bury that very night, before I lost my poor leg. And I quarreled with your grandf-, ha!"

As he said "Ha!" there came three quiet little taps on the table, it is the middle table in the "Gray's-Inn CoffeeHouse," under the bust of the late Duke of W-ll-ngt-n.

"I fired in the air," he continued; "did I not?" (Tap, tap, tap.) "Your grandfather hit me in the leg. He married three months afterwards. 'Captain Brown,' I said 'who could see Miss Sm-th without loving her?' She is there! She is there!" (Tap, tap, tap.) "Yes, my first love"

But here there came tap, tap, which everybody knows means "No."

"I forgot," he said, with a faint blush stealing over his wan features, "she was not my first love. In Germ-in my own country-there WAS a young woman-"

Tap, tap, tap. There was here quite a lively little treble knock; and when the old man said, "But I loved thee better than all the world, Eliza," the affirmative signal was briskly repeated.

And this I declare UPON MY HONOR. There was, I have said, a bottle of port wine before us, I should say a decanter. That decanter was LIFTED UP, and out of it into our respective glasses two bumpers of wine were poured. I appeal to Mr. Hart, the landlord. I appeal to James, the respectful and intelligent waiter, if this statement is not true? And when we had finished that magnum, and I said, for I did not now in the least doubt her presence "Dear gr-nny, may we have another magnum?" the table DISTINCTLY rapped "No.".

"Now, my good sir," Mr. Pinto said, who really began to be affected by the wine, "you understand the interest I have taken in you. I loved Eliza ----" (of course I don't mention family names). "I knew you had that box which belonged to her, I will give you what you like for that box. Name your price at once, and I pay you on the spot."

"Why, when you came out, you said you had not six-pence in your pocket."

"Bah! give you anything you like – fifty -a hundred - a tausend pound."

"Come, come," said I, "the gold of the box may be worth nine guineas, and the facon we will put at six more."

"One tausend guineas!" he screeched. "One tausend and fifty pound dere!" and he sank back in his chair no, by the way, on his bench, for he was sitting with his back to one of the partitions of the boxes, as I dare say James remembers.

"DON'T go on in this way," I continued rather weakly, for I did not know whether I was in a dream. "If you offer me a thousand guineas for this box I MUST take it. Mustn't I, dear gr-nny?"

The table most distinctly said "Yes"; and putting out his claws to seize the box, Mr. Pinto plunged his hooked nose into it, and eagerly inhaled some of my 47 with a dash of Hardman.

"But stay, you old harpy!" I exclaimed, being now in a sort of rage, and quite familiar with him. "Where is the money? Where is the check?"

"James, a piece of note paper and a receipt stamp!"

"This is all mighty well, sir," I said, "but I don't know you; I never saw you before. I will trouble you to hand me that box back again, or give me a check with some known signature."

"Whose? Ha, Ha, HA!"

The room happened to be very dark. Indeed all the waiters were gone to supper, and there were only two gentlemen snoring in their respective boxes. I saw a hand come quivering down from the ceiling, a very pretty hand, on which was a ring with a coronet, with a lion rampant gules for a crest. I saw that hand take a dip of ink and write across the paper. Mr. Pinto, then, taking a gray receipt stamp out of his blue leather pocketbook, fastened it on to the paper by the usual process; and the hand then wrote across the receipt stamp, went across the table and shook hands with Pinto, and then, as if waving him an adieu, vanished in the direction of the ceiling.

There was the paper before me, wet with the ink. There was the pen which THE HAND had used. Does anybody doubt me? I have that pen now, a cedar stick of a not uncommon sort, and holding one of Gillott's pens. It is in my inkstand now, I tell you. Anybody may see it. The handwriting on the check, for such the document was, was the writing of a female. It ran thus: "London, midnight, March 31, 1862. Pay the bearer one thousand and fifty pounds. Rachel Sidonia. To Messrs. Sidonia, Pozzosanto and Co., London."

"Noblest and best of women!" said Pinto, kissing the sheet of paper with much reverence. "My good Mr. Roundabout, I suppose you do not question THAT signature?"

Indeed the house of Sidonia, Pozzosanto and Co., is known to be one of the richest in Europe, and as for the Countess Rachel, she was known to be the chief manager of that enormously wealthy establishment. There was only one little difficulty, the Countess Rachel died last October.

I pointed out this circumstance, and tossed over the paper to Pinto with a sneer.

"C'est a brandre ou a laisser," he said with some heat. "You literary men are all imbrudent; but I did not tink you such a fool wie dis. Your box is not worth twenty pound, and I offer you a tausend because I know you want money to pay dat rascal Tom's college bills." (This strange man actually knew that my scapegrace Tom had been a source of great expense and annoyance to me.)

"You see money costs me nothing, and you refuse to take it! Once, twice; will you take this check in exchange for your trumpery snuff-box?"

What could I do? My poor granny's legacy was valuable and dear to me, but after all a thousand guineas are not to be had every day. "Be it a bargain," said I. "Shall we have a glass of wine on it?" says Pinto; and to this proposal I also unwillingly acceded, reminding him, by the way, that he had not yet told me the story of the headless man.

"Your poor grandmother was right just now, when she said she was not my first love. 'Twas one of those banale expressions" (here Mr. P. blushed once more) "which we use to women. We tell each she is our first passion. They reply with a similar illusory formula. No man is any woman's first love; no woman any man's. We are in love in our nurse's arms, and women coquette with their eyes before their tongue can form a word. How could your lovely relative love me? I was far, far too old for her. I am older than I look. I am so old that you would not believe my age were I to tell you. I have loved many and many a woman before your relative. It has not always been fortunate for them to love me. Ah, Sophronia! Round the dreadful circus where you fell, and whence I was dragged corpselike by the heels, there sat multitudes more savage than the lions which mangled your sweet form! Ah, tenez! when we marched to the terrible stake together at Valladolid the Protestant and the J - But away with memory! Boy! it was happy for thy grandam that she loved me not.

"During that strange period," he went on, "when the teeming Time was great with the revolution that was speedily to be born, I was on a mission in Paris with my excellent, my maligned friend, Cagliostro. Mesmer was one of our band. I seemed to occupy but an obscure rank in it: though, as you know, in secret societies the humble man may be a chief and director the ostensible leader but a puppet moved by unseen hands. Never mind who was chief, or who was second. Never mind my age. It boots not to tell it: why shall I expose myself to your scornful incredulity or reply to your questions in words that are familiar to you, but which you cannot understand? Words are symbols of things which you know, or of things which you don't know. If you don't know them, to speak is idle." (Here I confess Mr. P. spoke for exactly thirty-eight minutes, about physics, metaphysics, language, the origin and destiny of man, during which time I was rather bored, and to relieve my ennui, drank a half glass or so of wine.) "LOVE, friend, is the fountain of youth! It may not happen to me once - once in an age: but when I love then I am young. I loved when I was in Paris. Bathilde, Bathilde,

I loved thee, ah, how fondly! Wine, I say, more wine! Love is ever young. I was a boy at the little feet of Bathilde de Bechamel the fair, the fond, the fickle, ah, the false!" The strange old man's agony was here really terrific, and he showed himself much more agitated than when he had been speaking about my grandmother.

"I thought Blanche might love me. I could speak to her in the language of all countries, and tell her the lore of all ages. I could trace the nursery legends which she loved up to their Sanscrit source, and whisper to her the darkling mysteries of the Egyptian Magi. I could chant for her the wild chorus that rang in the disheveled Eleusinian revel: I could tell her and I would, the watchword never known but to one woman, the Saban Queen, which Hiram breathed in the abysmal ear of Solomon--You don't attend. Psha! you have drunk too much wine!" Perhaps I may as well own that I was NOT attending, for he had been carrying on for about fifty-seven minutes; and I don't like a man to have ALL the talk to himself.

"Blanche de Bechamel was wild, then, about this secret of Masonry. In early, early days I loved, I married a girl fair as Blanche, who, too, was tormented by curiosity, who, too, would peep into my closet, into the only secret guarded from her. A dreadful fate befell poor Fatima. An ACCIDENT shortened her life. Poor thing! she had a foolish sister who urged her on. I always told her to beware of Ann. She died. They said her brothers killed me. A gross falsehood. AM I dead? If I were, could I pledge you in this wine?"

"Was your name," I asked, quite bewildered, "was your name, pray, then, ever Blueb----?"

"Hush! the waiter will overhear you. Methought we were speaking of Blanche de Bechamel. I loved her, young man. My pearls, and diamonds, and treasure, my wit, my wisdom, my passion, I flung them all into the child's lap. I was a fool. Was strong Samson not as weak as I? Was Solomon the Wise much better when Balkis wheedled him? I said to the king. But enough of that, I spake of Blanche de Bechamel.

"Curiosity was the poor child's foible. I could see, as I talked to her, that her thoughts were elsewhere (as yours, my friend, have been absent once or twice to-night). To know the secret of Masonry was the wretched child's mad desire. With a thousand wiles, smiles, caresses, she strove to coax it from me - from ME - ha! ha!

"I had an apprentice - the son of a dear friend, who died by my side at Rossbach, when Soubise, with whose army I happened to be, suffered a dreadful defeat for neglecting my advice. The Young Chevalier Goby de Mouchy was glad enough to serve as my clerk, and help in some chemical experiments in which I was engaged with my friend Dr. Mesmer. Bathilde saw this young man. Since women were, has it not been their business to smile and deceive, to fondle and lure? Away! From the very first it has been so!" And as my companion spoke, he looked as wicked as the serpent that coiled round the tree, and hissed a poisoned counsel to the first woman.

"One evening I went, as was my wont, to see Blanche. She was radiant: she was wild with spirits: a saucy triumph blazed in her blue eyes. She talked, she rattled in her childish way. She uttered, in the course of her rhapsody, a hint, an intimation, so terrible that the truth flashed across me in a moment. Did I ask her? She would lie to me. But I knew how to make falsehood impossible. And I ordered her to go to sleep."

At this moment the clock (after its previous convulsions) sounded TWELVE. And as the new Editor* of the Cornhill Magazine and HE, I promise you, won't stand any nonsense will only allow seven pages, I am obliged to leave off at THE VERY MOST INTERESTING POINT OF THE STORY.

* Mr. Thackeray retired from the Editorship of the Cornhill Magazine in March, 1862

III
"Are you of our fraternity? I see you are not. The secret which Mademoiselle de Bechamel confided to me in her mad triumph and wild hoyden spirits, she was but a child, poor thing, poor thing, scarce fifteen; but I love them young, a folly not unusual with the old!" (Here Mr. Pinto thrust his knuckles into his hollow eyes; and, I am sorry to say, so little regardful was he of personal cleanliness, that his tears made streaks of white over his guarled dark hands.) "Ah, at fifteen, poor child, thy fate was terrible! Go to! It is not good to love me, friend. They prosper not who do. I divine you. You need not say what you are thinking"

In truth, I was thinking, if girls fall in love with this sallow, hook-nosed, glass-eyed, wooden-legged, dirty, hideous old man, with the sham teeth, they have a queer taste. THAT is what I was thinking.

"Jack Wilkes said the handsomest man in London had but half an hour's start of him. And, without vanity, I am scarcely uglier than Jack Wilkes. We were members of the same club at Medenham Abbey, Jack and I, and had many a merry night together. Well, sir, I, Mary of Scotland knew me but as a little hunchbacked music master; and yet, and yet, I think she was not indifferent to her David Riz and SHE came to misfortune. They all do, they all do!"

"Sir, you are wandering from your point!" I said, with some severity. For, really, for this old humbug to hint that he had been the baboon who frightened the club at Medenham, that he had been in the Inquisition at Valladolid, that under the name of D. Riz, as he called it, he had known the lovely Queen of Scots, was a LITTLE too much. "Sir," then I said, "you were speaking about a Miss Bechamel. I really have not time to hear all of your biography."

"Faith, the good wine gets into my head." (I should think so, the old toper! Four bottles all but two glasses.) "To return to poor Blanche. As I sat laughing, joking with her, she let slip a word, a little word, which filled me with dismay. Some one had told her a part of the Secret, the secret which has been divulged scarce thrice in three thousand years, the Secret of the Freemasons. Do you know what happens to those uninitiate who learn that secret? To those wretched men, the initiate who reveal it?"

As Pinto spoke to me, he looked through and through me with his horrible piercing glance, so that I sat quite uneasily on my bench. He continued: "Did I question her awake? I knew she would lie to me. Poor child! I loved her no less because I did not believe a word she said. I loved her blue eye, her golden hair, her delicious voice, that was true in song, though when she spoke, false as Eblis! You are aware that I possess in rather a remarkable degree what we have agreed to call the mesmeric power. I set the unhappy girl to sleep. THEN she was obliged to tell me all. It was as I had surmised. Goby de Mouchy, my wretched, besotted miserable secretary, in his visits to the chateau of the Marquis de Bechamel, who was one of our society, had seen Blanche.

I suppose it was because she had been warned that he was worthless, and poor, artful and a coward, she loved him. She wormed out of the besotted wretch the secrets of our Order. 'Did he tell you the NUMBER ONE?' I asked.

"She said, 'Yes.'

"'Did he,' I further inquired, 'tell you the-'

"'Oh, don't ask me, don't ask me!' she said, writhing on the sofa, where she lay in the presence of the Marquis de Bechamel, her most unhappy father. Poor Bechamel, poor Bechamel! How pale he looked as I spoke! 'Did he tell you,' I repeated with a dreadful calm, 'the NUMBER TWO?' She said, 'Yes.'

"The poor old marquis rose up, and clasping his hands, fell on his knees before Count Cagl---- Bah! I went by a different name then. Vat's in a name? Dat vich ye call a Rosicrucian by any other name vil smell as sveet. 'Monsieur,' he said, 'I am old, I am rich. I have five hundred thousand livres of rentes in Picardy. I have half as much in Artois. I have two hundred and eighty thousand on the Grand Livre. I am promised by my Sovereign a dukedom and his orders with a reversion to my heir. I am a Grandee of Spain of the First Class, and Duke of Volovento. Take my titles, my ready money, my life, my honor, everything I have in the world, but don't ask the THIRD QUESTION.'

"'Godfroid de Bouillon, Comte de Bechamel, Grandee of Spain and Prince of Volovento, in our Assembly what was the oath you swore?' The old man writhed as he remembered its terrific purport.

"Though my heart was racked with agony, and I would have died, aye, cheerfully" (died, indeed, as if THAT were a penalty!) "to spare yonder lovely child a pang, I said to her calmly, 'Blanche de Bechamel, did Goby de Mouchy tell you secret NUMBER THREE?'

"She whispered a oui that was quite faint, faint and small. But her poor father fell in convulsions at her feet.

"She died suddenly that night. Did I not tell you those I love come to no good? When General Bonaparte crossed the Saint Bernard, he saw in the convent an old monk with a white beard, wandering about the corridors, cheerful and rather stout, but mad, mad as a March hare. 'General,' I said to him, 'did you ever see that face before?' He had not. He had not mingled much with the higher classes of our society before the Revolution. I knew the poor old man well enough; he was the last of a noble race, and I loved his child."

"And did she die by - ?"

"Man! did I say so? Do I whisper the secrets of the Vehmgericht? I say she died that night: and he, he, the heartless, the villain, the betrayer, you saw him seated in yonder curiosity shop, by yonder guillotine, with his scoundrelly head in his lap.

"You saw how slight that instrument was? It was one of the first which Guillotin made, and which he showed to private friends in a hangar in the Rue Picpus, where he lived. The invention created some little conversation among scientific men at the time, though I remember a machine in Edinburgh of a very similar construction, two hundred, well, many, many years ago and at a breakfast which Guillotin gave he showed us the instrument, and much talk arose among us as to whether people suffered under it.

"And now I must tell you what befell the traitor who had caused all this suffering. Did he know that the poor child's death was a SENTENCE? He felt a cowardly satisfaction that with her was gone the secret of his treason. Then he began to doubt. I had MEANS to penetrate all his thoughts, as well as to know his acts. Then he became a slave to a horrible fear. He fled in abject terror to a convent. They still existed in Paris; and behind the walls of Jacobins the wretch thought himself secure. Poor fool! I had but to set one of my somnambulists to sleep. Her spirit went forth and spied the shuddering wretch in his cell. She described the street, the gate, the convent, the very dress which he wore, and which you saw to-day.

"And now THIS is what happened. In his chamber in the Rue St. Honore, at Paris, sat a man ALONE a man who has been maligned, a man who has been called a knave and charlatan, a man who has been persecuted even to the death, it is said, in Roman Inquisitions, forsooth, and elsewhere. Ha! ha! A man who has a mighty will.

"And looking toward the Jacobins Convent (of which, from his chamber, he could see the spires and trees), this man WILLED. And it was not yet dawn. And he willed; and one who was lying in his cell in the convent of Jacobins, awake and shuddering with terror for a crime which he had committed, fell asleep.

"But though he was asleep his eyes were open.

"And after tossing and writhing, and clinging to the pallet, and saying 'No, I will not go,' he rose up and donned his clothes, a gray coat, a vest of white pique, black satin small-clothes, ribbed silk stockings, and a white stock with a steel buckle; and he arranged his hair, and he tied his queue, all the while being in that strange somnolence which walks, which moves, which FLIES sometimes, which sees, which is indifferent to pain, which OBEYS. And he put on his hat, and he went forth from his cell: and though the dawn was not yet, he trod the corridors as seeing them. And he passed into the cloister, and then into the garden where lie the ancient dead. And he came to the wicket, which Brother Jerome was opening just at the dawning. And the crowd was already waiting with their cans and bowls to receive the alms of the good brethren.

"And he passed through the crowd and went on his way, and the few people then abroad who marked him, said, 'Tiens! How very odd he looks! He looks like a man walking in his sleep!' This was said by various persons:-

"By milk women, with their cans and carts, coming into the town.

"By roysterers who had been drinking at the taverns of the Barrier, for it was Mid-Lent.

"By the sergeants of the watch, who eyed him sternly as he passed near their halberds.

"But he passed on unmoved by their halberds,

"Unmoved by the cries of the roysterers,

"By the market women coming with their milk and eggs.

"He walked through the Rue St. Honore, I say:-

"By the Rue Rambuteau,

"By the Rue St. Antoine,

"By the King's Chateau of the Bastille,

"By the Faubourg St. Antoine.

"And he came to No. 29 in the Rue Picpus a house which then stood between a court and garden

"That is, there was a building of one story, with a great coach door.

"Then there was a court, around which were stables, coach-houses, offices.

"Then there was a house, a two-storied house, with a perron in front.

"Behind the house was a garden, a garden of two hundred and fifty French feet in length.

"And as one hundred feet of France equal one hundred and six feet of England, this garden, my friend, equaled exactly two hundred and sixty-five feet of British measure.

"In the center of the garden was a fountain and a statue or, to speak more correctly, two statues. One was recumbent, a man. Over him, saber in hand, stood a Woman.

"The man was Olofernes. The woman was Judith. From the head, from the trunk, the water gushed. It was the taste of the doctor:- was it not a droll of taste?

"At the end of the garden was the doctor's cabinet of study. My faith, a singular cabinet, and singular pictures!

"Decapitation of Charles Premier at Vitehall.

"Decapitation of Montrose at Edimbourg.

"Decapitation of Cinq Mars. When I tell you that he was a man of taste, charming!

"Through this garden, by these statues, up these stairs, went the pale figure of him who, the porter said, knew the way of the house. He did. Turning neither right nor left, he seemed to walk THROUGH the statues, the obstacles, the flower beds, the stairs, the door, the tables, the chairs.

"In the corner of the room was THAT INSTRUMENT, which Guillotin had just invented and perfected. One day he was to lay his own head under his own ax. Peace be to his name! With him I deal not!

"In a frame of mahogany, neatly worked, was a board with a half circle in it, over which another board fitted. Above was a heavy ax, which fell - you know how. It was held up by a rope, and when this rope was untied, or cut, the steel fell.

"To the story which I now have to relate, you may give credence, or not, as you will. The sleeping man went up to that instrument.

"He laid his head in it, asleep."

"Asleep?"

"He then took a little penknife out of the pocket of his white dimity waistcoat.

"He cut the rope asleep.

"The ax descended on the head of the traitor and villain. The notch in it was made by the steel buckle of his stock, which was cut through.

"A strange legend has got abroad that after the deed was done, the figure rose, took the head from the basket, walked forth through the garden, and by the screaming porters at the gate, and went and laid itself down at the Morgue. But for this I will not vouch. Only of this be sure. 'There are more things in heaven and earth, Horatio, than are dreamed of in your philosophy.' More and more the light peeps through the chinks. Soon, amidst music ravishing, the curtain will rise, and the glorious scene be displayed. Adieu! Remember me. Ha! 'tis dawn," Pinto said. And he was gone.

I am ashamed to say that my first movement was to clutch the check which he had left with me, and which I was determined to present the very moment the bank opened. I know the importance of these things, and that men change their mind sometimes. I sprang through the streets to the great banking house of

Manasseh in Duke Street. It seemed to me as if I actually flew as I walked. As the clock struck ten I was at the counter and laid down my check.

The gentleman who received it, who was one of the Hebrew persuasion, as were the other two hundred clerks of the establishment, having looked at the draft with terror in his countenance, then looked at me, then called to himself two of his fellow clerks, and queer it was to see all their aquiline beaks over the paper.

"Come, come!" said I, "don't keep me here all day. Hand me over the money, short, if you please!" for I was, you see, a little alarmed, and so determined to assume some extra bluster.

"Will you have the kindness to step into the parlor to the partners?" the clerk said, and I followed him.

"What, AGAIN?" shrieked a bald-headed, red-whiskered gentleman, whom I knew to be Mr. Manasseh. "Mr. Salathiel, this is too bad! Leave me with this gentleman, S." And the clerk disappeared.

"Sir," he said, "I know how you came by this: the Count de Pinto gave it you. It is too bad! I honor my parents; I honor THEIR parents; I honor their bills! But this one of grandma's is too bad - it is, upon my word, now! She've been dead these five-and-thirty years. And this last four months she has left her burial place and took to drawing on our 'ouse! It's too bad, grandma; it is too bad!" and he appealed to me, and tears actually trickled down his nose.

"Is it the Countess Sidonia's check or not?" I asked, haughtily.

"But, I tell you, she's dead! It's a shame! it's a shame! it is, grandmamma!" and he cried, and wiped his great nose in his yellow pocket handkerchief. "Look year, will you take pounds instead of guineas? She's dead, I tell you! It's no go! Take the pounds, one tausend pound! ten nice, neat, crisp hundred-pound notes, and go away vid you, do!"

"I will have my bond, sir, or nothing," I said; and I put on an attitude of resolution which I confess surprised even myself.

"Wery veil," he shrieked, with many oaths, "then you shall have Noting ha, ha, ha! noting but a policeman! Mr. Abednego, call a policeman! Take that, you humbug and impostor!" and here with an abundance of frightful language which I dare not repeat, the wealthy banker abused and defied me.

Au bout du compte, what was I to do, if a banker did not choose to honor a check drawn by his dead grandmother? I began to wish I had my snuff-box back. I began to think I was a fool for changing that little old-fashioned gold for this slip of strange paper.

Meanwhile the banker had passed from his fit of anger to a paroxysm of despair. He seemed to be addressing some person invisible, but in the room: "Look here, ma'am, you've really been coming it too strong. A hundred thousand in six onths, and now a thousand more! The 'ouse can't stand it; it WON'T stand it, I say! What? Oh! mercy, mercy!

As he uttered these words, A HAND fluttered over the table in the air! It was a female hand: that which I had seen the night before. That female hand took a pen from the green baize table, dipped it in a silver inkstand, and wrote on a quarter of a sheet of foolscap on the blotting book, "How about the diamond robbery? If you do not pay, I will tell him where they are."

What diamonds? what robbery? what was this mystery? That will never be ascertained, for the wretched man's demeanor instantly changed. "Certainly, sir; oh, certainly," he said, forcing a grin. "How will you have the money, sir? All right, Mr. Abednego. This way out."

"I hope I shall often see you again," I said; on which I own poor Manasseh gave a dreadful grin, and shot back into his parlor.

I ran home, clutching the ten delicious, crisp hundred pounds, and the dear little fifty which made up the account. I flew through the streets again. I got to my chambers. I bolted the outer doors. I sank back in my great chair, and slept. . . .

My first thing on waking was to feel for my money. Perdition! Where was I? Ha! on the table before me was my grandmother's snuff-box, and by its side one of those awful, those admirable, sensation novels, which I had been reading, and which are full of delicious wonder.

But that the guillotine is still to be seen at Mr. Gale's, No. 47, High Holborn, I give you MY HONOR. I suppose I was dreaming about it. I don't know. What is dreaming? What is life? Why shouldn't I sleep on the ceiling? and am I sitting on it now, or on the floor? I am puzzled. But enough. If the fashion for sensation novels goes on, I tell you I will write one in fifty volumes. For the present, DIXI. But between ourselves, this Pinto, who fought at the Colosseum, who was nearly being roasted by the Inquisition, and sang duets at Holyrood, I am rather sorry to lose him after three little bits of Roundabout Papers. Et vous?

www.ingramcontent.com/pod-product-compliance
Lightning Source LLC
Chambersburg PA
CBHW061456170626
46811CB00004B/1541